ABOUT THE AUTHOR

Eric Grate was born in Greenfield, OH, and raised in its tough South End. He is a 1984 graduate of Edward Lee McClain High School and a veteran of the United States Marine Corps. He worked in the automotive industry as a Quality Engineer for twenty years, owned and operated a successful portrait studio for eleven years, and owns and operates Big Jack's Coffeehouse & Café with two locations in Lawrenceburg, KY. Eric resides in Danville, KY, with his wife, Michelle, and their mean cat, Boo Radley.

The Streets of Greenfield

Eric Grate

First edition, November 2023

E.C. Grate Creative Content, LLC
dba Coal Shed Publishing Company
Danville, KY USA

ISBN: 979-8-9883716-0-1 (Paperback)
ISBN: 979-8-9883716-1-8 (Hardcover)

Book Cover design by Michelle Grate

www.ericgrate.com

Printed in the United States of America

For my wife, Michelle. You are the love of my life and my biggest supporter.

Thank you for helping me realize that I could really do this.

For my brother, Keith (Lucky). Every boy needs a hero. You were mine.

Thank you for pushing me along when I wasn't sure I'd make it.

"You can't blame a writer for what the characters say."
    – Truman Capote

Contents

PHONE 275-R

WANTED: Man to dig a hole. Must have a shovel. Tarp and lunch provided. Phone 275-R. (Greenfield)

A LETTER FROM THE OHIO PENITENTIARY

January 1, 1957

Allen Wayne Delaney
Inmate # 3812051X
Ohio Penitentiary
Columbus, Ohio

Mrs. Iva Delaney
Route 3
Greenfield, Ohio

Dear Momma,

Happy New Year!

I was lying awake last night wondering if you were at Aunt Eileen's house ringing in the new year. I always loved going to her house on New Year's when I was a boy, even if I always fell asleep before midnight. There isn't much celebrating here, not at New Year's or any other time.

I want you to know that I received the cookies you and Granny sent at Christmas. Most of them, anyway. I know the guards had their share before the box got to me. No matter. There were at least a dozen chocolate chip and sugar cookies in the box when I got it. I had them all in one sitting!

There is a new Captain in charge of the unit. He came in last Tuesday. His name is Gallina. Big square jawed Italian guy. They say he was a Marine and fought on Guadalcanal. I have to say that he doesn't seem like a terrible fellow. We are supposed to be in our cells every night by nine o'clock, but he will sometimes allow us to stay in the common area until nine-twenty or even nine-thirty as long as everyone is acting right and keeping the noise down. Twenty or thirty extra minutes might not sound like much. But every minute outside that tiny cell is a gift.

I hope you're doing well, Momma. Is your ankle still swollen? I told you about walking up those steps after you've been drinking! I'm only joking. I hope you are healing up.

Did Margie Dickinson have her baby yet? It wouldn't surprise me one bit if that baby looked more like a Kessler than a Dickinson. HAHAHA! Don't say anything, though. Old Pete might die!

Do you remember Clyde Duckett? He's John Duckett's son. John was our mailman when we lived on Paint Street. Me and Clyde were friends in third grade. Anyway, I got a letter from him a few days ago. He lives up around Canton now, but he heard about my situation and wanted me to know he was praying for me. He said he always liked me when we were kids. I never cared much about praying before, but I pray every day now. I say the Lord's Prayer just like you taught me when I was little.

Momma, I have something to tell you and it breaks my heart to write it. I suspect you already know, but I want to say it to clear my conscience. I did the things they say I did. All of them. It hurts my soul for you to have to hear that. I'm sorry for saying I didn't do it. I guess a man will say just about anything to try to save his skin. It's past that now, though. I'm very sorry for what I did. Not just sorry for myself but for his parents and his sisters. I hope they will have peace and comfort when this is all finished. I'm also sorry for you and our family. I guess it's hard for you to go anywhere in Greenfield and not see people staring and hear them whispering. I'm really sad about causing that. I'm telling you this because when I'm gone, I don't want you to spend your remaining years thinking that your son was done wrong. That might make you hate the people who sent me to this place. It's not their fault, though. It's my fault, Momma. Don't hate anyone. I know you won't hate your son.

When he's old enough to understand, I want you to tell little Morris that his cousin said never to gamble at cards. If he must gamble at all, ask him to gamble at pool. A man shooting pool is just having fun because it's just a game. No man feeds his family by shooting pool. Shooting pool can put a few quarters in your pocket, but playing cards is a different story. It's the devil's business. Playing cards can keep food on the table if a man is good enough. It can also consume a man's spirit and lead him down a path of ruin. Bill Stumloski told me and Donnie Lytle that one time when we were kids hanging around outside the pool hall. I didn't pay any attention when he said it, but I know what he meant now.

Momma, this will be my last letter. In eight more days, I will be no more for this Earth. I will be living my eternal life with Jesus and the saints. I'm excited to see my sister, Grace, whom I never met. Will she still be a newborn baby? I'll hug her and tell her how much you love her and how you've never forgotten her.

I won't lie, Momma. I wish I could walk the streets of Greenfield just once more. Maybe I'd take some different turns this time. It's okay though because soon, I will be walking the streets of glory!

You must understand that nothing you did or didn't do brought me to this end, Momma. You raised me and taught me right from wrong. You have been the best mother in the world and no blame rests on your shoulders. I chose to do bad things on my own. No one could have stopped me except the Lord himself, and he saw fit to let me do what I wanted to do.

I'm trying to stay busy so my mind doesn't get overwhelmed with feelings of dread. A pair of cardinals sit in the tree outside my window every morning and sing. It's the only tree in the yard and sits just fifteen or twenty feet outside my cell window. Did I ever tell you that? Anyway, I enjoy watching those birds and listening to their pretty songs. There's some sewing that needs doing on the inseam of a pair of pants and I have several socks that need darning. I hope I have time to finish reading "Sweet Thursday." It's a John Steinbeck book. There are seventy-seven pages left. I think I can do it.

I was thinking yesterday what I wanted for my last meal. I thought about pork chops, meatloaf, or fried chicken, but they wouldn't be nearly as good as yours, so I settled on a big bag of Carrol's potato chips, a block of Colby cheese, and an ice-cold Double Cola.

It would be best if you didn't come to visit the day before. It would hurt me too much to see your worried face. I want to remember you like when we were together at home. I can see you standing in the kitchen in your apron, baking pies and singing to the Lord. That's how I want to picture you, Momma, as I take my last breath on Earth.

I hope you'll remember me sitting on the porch in the evenings, playing my guitar and drinking sweet tea in my sock feet. Those were the happiest times for me.

Tell Granny goodbye for me, although she won't understand. Tell her I love her. And say goodbye to my cousins, aunts, uncles, and friends.

Oh, my dear, sweet Momma. It's time for me to kiss your cheek and tell you goodbye. I wish I could be there to comfort you. I miss you so much, but will see you again in paradise.

Remember me as I was, not as I am.

Your loving son,

Allen

P.S. There is a pocketknife in the cigar box on the dresser in my old bedroom. Please give that to Morris. You can do however you see fit with the rest of my belongings. I don't reckon they are worth much. - A

COLTRANE

"Coltrane! How many times have I told you not to come in here? Huh? Are you deaf or somethin'? Now, turn your smelly carcass around and get the Hell out."

George Ambrose Coltrane IV. A man largely forgotten by the world didn't say a word. He simply tipped his hat, bowed, and backed out the door. "They won't get any more of my business," he said from the sidewalk along Jefferson Street. "No, sir! Not another dime's worth." Coltrane looked at the sign over the door. "The Guest House. I need to write that down," he said, searching his coat pockets for a notebook and pencil that didn't exist. Giving up, Coltrane stood up straight, smoothed his jacket, jabbed his finger into the air, and said with conviction, "I'm boycotting you starting right now!" Then he executed a wobbly right face and marched up the street.

The cold wind stung his face as he walked past the storefronts decorated with Christmas lights and wreaths. A light snow fell, and Coltrane covered his ears with his hands as he walked along. The distant rumble of what sounded like thunder rolled in from the east. "Did you hear that?" Coltrane asked a young couple walking by.

The man eyed him suspiciously, and the woman stepped behind her beau. "I didn't hear anything, mister." Looking Coltrane up and down, the man continued, "I think you better get home and sleep it off."

Coltrane cocked his ear to the left and heard it again. It sounded like thunder or just something similar, perhaps.

"Coltrane!"

"Yessir!"

"Coltrane, I need you to take five men and clear the goddamn Germans out of that wood line. That machine gun is tearing us to shreds."

"Yessir! Updike, Lieberman, Wilson, Smith, Mills. Come with me."

When he got to the center of town, Coltrane leaned against a light post and waved at the police car as it went by. Then, he reached into his coat pocket and retrieved the bottle of Muscatel he had hidden away. He took a long drink, smacked his lips, and crossed the street.

Coltrane stopped on the opposite corner and stood at attention while Taps played in his head. He snapped a somewhat sharp salute to the monument standing beside city hall. The gallant Rainbow Division had marched off to fight the Hun nearly fifty years before and win the war to end all wars. American men would never have to go off to foreign lands ever again to spill blood and have blood spilled. Of course, the history books tell us otherwise.

"Listen up! I want us to fix bayonets. Fill your pockets with cartridges and carry an extra grenade. Get one off your buddy if you need to."

"Wilson! Mills! Circle around to the right, beyond those dead cows, and move through the woods to within twenty-five yards of that

Machine gun. Don't open fire until you hear our fire from the front. Advance through the woods and get close enough to use your grenades. You got it?"

Coltrane finished his salute, and, almost as if on cue, the bells from St. Benignus came to life and let Greenfield know that it was 10:00 pm. The sharp report from the bell cut through the cold air and reverberated off buildings.

After taking another drink of Muscatel, Coltrane started down Washington Street at a deliberate pace, singing chopped-up verses of "Lonely Blue Boy" and drinking from his concealed bottle of wine. When he got to Johnny's Eight Ball, he stopped and approached the door.

"Don't even think about it, old buddy," said the burly man smoking a cigarette by the door. "Keep movin'."

Coltrane groaned and moved along.

"Updike and Smith. You make for that pile of rocks off to the left. Be sure you're well covered and concealed. Don't fire until me and Lieberman do. Understand? Lieberman, you stay with me. We're going to occupy that big shell hole to our front. We'll lay down a good fire and get the Krauts to focus on us. That's when you other four advance and give 'em Hell. We'll attack from the front as soon as you start your attacks on the flanks. Questions? Good! Let's move!"

Coltrane continued walking. The Furio's Pizza car sped past on a delivery, and the driver honked the horn. Coltrane threw his hand up and waved.

"Let 'em have it! Keep firing! Okay, pour it on 'em, Lieberman! Let's go! Stay low! Make for the wall in front! Shit! Lieberman! Lieberman! Dammit!"

Coltrane could hear music coming from up ahead at The Huddle, and he made his way towards it, singing along with George Jones and stopping at one point to tap his foot and strum his imaginary guitar.

Making sure no one was looking, Coltrane slipped in the door and sat at the bar before anyone realized he was there. No one seemed to notice, but one woman did pick up her drink and retreat to a table in the back.

"Coltrane. What the Hell, man? You know you ain't supposed to be in here. You're gonna get my ass fired."

Ahh, come on, Bill. Just one drink."

"It's Phil, and you're loaded already. You've had enough."

"Just one, my friend, and I'll be off to my mansion on the hill."

"Shit! I'm gonna serve you one drink. Then, out you go. You understand?"

"I'll have a double bourbon on the rocks, my good man. Old Grandad, if you please."

The bartender looked suspiciously at the old man. "You got money?"

"I got my relief check yesterday."

The bartender poured the drink. "You smell like a barn. You know that, right?"

"You dirty bastards! Eat that, you motherfuckers!" Wilson! Over here! Concentrate your fire. Give 'em the grenades! Updike! You and Smith. Keep moving! That's it, boys. We got 'em!"

Coltrane removed his hat and looked around. In the mirror behind the bar, he saw a familiar face. It was an old man. His father, maybe? Coltrane smiled and nodded. The old man did likewise, and they tipped back their drinks together.

"Alright, Coltrane," the bartender said, "Time to shove off."

"How about one on the house?"

"Not a snowball's chance in Hell. The next thing you know, you'll be lyin' on the floor, pissin' yourself and goin' on about Nazis and Lieberman or whatever the Hell his name is. Cryin' and moanin'. No one wants to hear that shit while they're tryin' to relax. Now scat. And don't forget to pay for the drink."

The bartender returned to his duties while Coltrane put on his hat and stood up. There was pain in his shoulder and in both legs. It felt familiar, like a memory. Reaching into his pocket, Coltrane took out two pieces of silver. One a dollar and one a star. He laid the star on the bar and put the dollar back in his pocket. Then he walked out into the cold night.

"What about Lieberman? Did he make it? Am I gonna lose my legs? Did we take out that machine gun? Aaagghhh! My shoulder! For the love of God!"

Coltrane walked along the railroad tracks, hands in pockets, trying to ignore the sounds in his head. He realized long ago they weren't real. If he ignored them long enough, they'd go away, like the pain in his shoulder and legs. It always went away.

When he reached the trestle, he picked up his pace. It was a long walk to Thrifton, and he just remembered a bottle he had hidden in a hole in a tree before Bonnie left. Surely, it was still there. *How long ago was that now*, he wondered. *It must have been three years. At least three years.*

He heard a rumble in the distance when he got a quarter way across the trestle.

"Listen. Vehicles approaching."

Coltrane stopped and shook his head, trying to get the noise out. He pulled the bottle from his pocket and drained the Muscatel down his throat before tossing it off the trestle and into the dark.

"Keep moving! Stay to the side."

Coltrane started his walk again and listened for the creek rapids running below, but the rumble drowned them out.

"Panzers!"

There was a sudden blast of wind and a screech of tank tracks. No, train wheels. It was train wheels. There were no panzers. There was only the nine o'clock train out of Middletown heading to Chillicothe, and it was right on schedule.

As Coltrane went over the edge and started the last few seconds of his life, he thought once more of Lieberman and that time in Belgium. He thought of the lives he saved and the lives he took. He had endured twenty years with the former and would now spend eternity with the latter. "It's just another adventure," Coltrane said out loud. "It's just another adventure."

"Coltrane! Coltrane!"

THE CARNIVAL

Ten-year-old David Tuttle sits in front of his bedroom window, looking dejected. His life's savings: a crisp five-dollar bill, three worn one-dollar bills, a stack of four quarters, and a few dimes, nickels, and pennies lay on the desk before him. David counts the money and whispers, "Nine dollars and thirty-four cents." *It should be more,* he thinks.

Just over six months ago, as the calendar flipped to 1976, David had resolved to save all his money for the carnival set up this very minute just a few blocks away. At five dollars per week allowance, ten-cent memory verses at church, random odd jobs around the neighborhood, and loose change picked up here and there, that should have been at least two hundred dollars. Instead, his appetite for Saturday matinees at the Rand Theater, baseball cards, ice cream cones, Bubble Yum, and records from the Sundry Store has left him with a measly nine dollars and thirty-four cents.

"Shit," David mumbles, his shoulders slumped forward in despair. He thinks for a moment, trying to remember any sources of untapped funding that may have slipped his mind. Then he jumps up and runs out of his bedroom, down the hallway, and into the bathroom. He opens the laundry basket and digs past his dirty baseball uniform, various smelly socks, and a couple damp hand towels. Picking up a pair of his dad's Dickies, David shoves his hands into the pockets. Nothing. Next are a pair of Eddie's grimy blue jeans. David searches the pockets and finds a condom, a quarter, and a neatly folded one-dollar bill. Grinning, he drops the condom in the hamper and stuffs the bill and quarter into his front pocket. His mom's pink gardening shorts produce nothing but a used Kleenex and a bottle cap, and her "Kiss The Cook" apron is barren except for a piece of orange peel in the pocket. The Kleenex, bottle cap, and orange peel go back into the hamper, along with the dirty clothes. Satisfied with his take, David runs back to his room.

Sitting down at his desk, David counts his money again. Ten dollars and fifty-nine cents. *That's a little more like it,* he thinks. Not a fortune by any stretch, but enough to have a good time if he spends wisely and doesn't get caught up shooting at cards with BB guns or tossing ping pong balls at goldfish bowls. He's always been a sucker for those games but is determined to resist them this year. David folds the bills, sticks them in his wallet, and slips it into his back pocket. The change goes into his right pocket, and his Kamp King pocketknife into his left.

Trying to avoid a lecture, David slips quietly down the steps and attempts to pass unnoticed by the kitchen, where his mother is clipping coupons.

"Wait! Come here, David," a familiar voice commands.

David stops, shakes his head, mumbles under his breath, and walks into the kitchen.

"Now, don't forget," his mother says, not looking up from her work. "You're going straight there. No stopping off anywhere on the way."

"I won't, Mom," David promises.

"Don't waste your money on nonsense," his mother advises. "Those goldfish they give away as prizes. They won't live two days. And I swear, David," she says while looking at him over her glasses and pointing a finger, "if you bring home one of those awful mirrors with marijuana leaves or half-naked girls on it, I'll break it over your head. Do you hear me, mister?"

"Gosh, Mom. Yes!" David answers, shifting back and forth on his feet. "Can I go now, before they pack up and leave town?"

His mother smiles. "Have fun, and don't get in any trouble. Be home by nine-thirty. I'll order pizza for you and Herbie. I might even bake some cookies."

"Thanks, Mom," David says as he leans over and kisses her on the cheek.

"I love you, Hunny," Mrs. Tuttle says.

"I love you too," David replies as he turns to go.

David walks out the door, down the steps, and across the yard. He turns up Spring Street and instinctively avoids cracks in the sidewalk so as not to break his mother's back. He waves at Mrs. Adams standing in her yard across the street. She's too busy talking to her rose bushes to notice, though, and pays him no mind.

The carnival had come to town Tuesday, but it had rained all that day and most of the next, so it was Thursday before things really got going. Still, his mother made David wait until Friday to go because it was *"Nothing but a mud hole,"* and she didn't want him ruining his shoes.

After the carnival, David and Herbie Farmer are

coming back to David's house for a sleepover. They'll have pizza and watch "Scars of Dracula," on Nite Owl Theater, in David's room. David might even smuggle in a dirty magazine from his dad's hidden stash in the garage.

David and Herbie have been friends since the Farmers' moved to Greenfield from Indiana two years ago. Herbie was given the new kid treatment by the other boys, but David, drawn to the Official NFL Wilson football that Herbie had brought to school on his first day, befriended him from the start. Theirs became the classic boys' friendship. Riding bicycles all over town, movie matinees at The Rand, fishing in Hovis Pond, pickup baseball games, sleepovers, late-night manhunts, and backyard campouts.

Herbie acts as the thinker and planner of the duo. Cautious, he tends to see the bigger picture, and he considers the consequences of his actions. Thus, he can keep himself, and David for that matter, out of trouble most of the time.

David, on the other hand, is more impetuous. He lives for the moment and sometimes pays the price for his actions. This means that Herbie sometimes pays the price for David's actions too.

When he gets to the alley by Schrader's Market, David crosses the street and hangs a right on Eighth. It's hot and muggy from all the rain that has fallen, and many of the yards need mowing. He thinks about pushing the mower around the neighborhood this weekend and trying to make a few bucks.

The carnival is Greenfield's premier social event of the year. Every June, just after school lets out for summer, it pulls into town and sets up in what the locals call the practice field because it's where the McClain High School football team practices. The field covers an entire city block bordered by McClain Avenue to the north, North Street to the south, Seventh Street to the east, and Eighth Street to the west. In the northwest corner is the old ball field, where the local baseball teams played before Don Grate Municipal Field was built last year on the edge of town.

David's senses kick in as he approaches the field. The smell of fried fish sandwiches, funnel cakes, and buttered popcorn mingles with the sounds of the Merry-Go-Round calliope, Bumper Car buzzers, and "Saturday Night" by the Bay City Rollers coming from The Scat.

As he strolls through the maze of rides and games, David thinks about how he wants to spend his money. The scrawny old guy with hooks for hands that runs the Quarter Pusher is scary as hell, but the lure of those shiny Zippo lighters is just too much to resist. He'll spend a dollar there and try to win one for sure. Throwing balls at milk cans seems safe. He couldn't think of how they could cheat at that, so he'll play a couple games and try to win a switchblade comb or maybe some Chinese thumb cuffs. He decides to skip the shooting games since he knows they bend the sights on the rifles and the ring toss because he has never seen anyone win. Although he likes the duck pond, he's afraid the other boys will see him playing and call him a pussy. After all, he's almost eleven years old. He'll walk through the House of Mirrors and maybe the Spook House, as long as Herbie isn't too chicken shit. The rides are easy. If it goes fast or high, it's a go. The Scat, the Swings, Ferris Wheel, and Tilt-A-Whirl are all good, as are the Bumper Cars and maybe even the Merry-Go-Round. There is only one show this year, "Gorilla Girl." His dad took him to see it when he was six years old, and it scared him so bad that he cried when the girl turned into a gorilla and ripped the door from her cage. He thinks he'll give it another shot and try to redeem himself. When it comes to food, he'll have a candied apple and maybe some french fries. If he runs into his Aunt Mary, he might ask her to buy him a Coke.

David checks his watch. It's four - seventeen. He's meeting Herbie in front of the Ferris Wheel at four-thirty, so he starts walking that way.

As he approaches the Ferris Wheel, the operator, a skinny man named Lester with a ponytail and fu Manchu mustache, motions for David to come near. "Hey, kid," Lester says. "I'll give you a free spin if you walk over there and get me a lemonade," pointing towards the Greenfield Mother's Club stand next to the Flying Elephants.

David looks at the top of the Ferris Wheel and then at Lester. "Will you stop it at the top for a couple minutes so I can look around?"

"Sure. No problem," Lester replies as he pulls a roll of sweaty one-dollar bills from the pocket of his cut-off jean shorts and hands one to David.

David walks quickly to the lemonade stand, places the order, slips the change into his pocket, and brings Lester his lemonade.

"Gracias," Lester says while removing the lid and straw from the Styrofoam cup and throwing them on the ground. He puts the cup to his mouth and takes a big gulp of lemonade. "Mmmmmmm-mmm, that's some good shit," he says, wiping his mouth with the back of his hand. "Climb on board, my friend."

There is no line, so David walks up the ramp, steps into the silver car, and sits down. He gets a whiff of body odor as Lester pulls the safety bar down over his lap and pins it in place. The fingers of Lester's right hand have LOVE tattooed on them in dark green ink, and the fingers of his left hand have MATE. David chuckles.

A giant wad of purple bubblegum is stuck to the right side of the car, and a half-eaten Blow Pop, covered in flies, lies on the footrest. David reaches out with the toe of his shoe and flicks the sucker onto the grass.

"OK, buddy. Here we go," Lester says.

David watches as Lester turns a key on the control panel and pulls the long lever to start the ride. There's a bump, followed by the sound of grinding gears, and the big wheel starts to move. David grips the bar with both hands and grins as he moves skyward. After three or four revolutions, the ride slows to a halt at the top.

Looking towards the intersection of Seventh and McClain, David watches a white Plymouth Duster with a Furio's Pizza sign on top making a delivery. A group of kids is crossing the street and walking down the grassy hill toward the carnival. He recognizes some of them, including Teddy Morrow, the best pitcher in Greenfield Little League.

Off to the right, he can see up the alley toward Herbie's house on Lafayette Street. Herbie's bicycle is lying in the corner of their yard, and his mom's blue Pinto is just pulling into the driveway. Crazy old Emo Gottlieb is walking up the alley with his burlap bag of pop bottles slung over his shoulder, and a white-haired woman wearing a red apron is in her backyard poking at her burning trash can with a stick.

To his left, David can see the rides, games, and food booths laid out before him. He watches as the Scat starts to spin and hears the screams of the riders as they carry across the field. He sees three-hundred-pound Marylin Trainor sitting on her reserved bench on the Merry-Go-Round. She has short salt and pepper hair and wears Coke bottle glasses, orthopedic shoes, and a sleeveless dress as big as a tent. She almost has a royal air about her, holding court while little kids and their parents board to ride. Marylin nods and returns greetings in a whisper. She rides all day and all night. Hundreds of revolutions. Around and around. She has played the same part for as long as most people can remember. The line at the Fire Department's fish fry tent is eight or ten deep. David's third-grade teacher, Miss Buddwalk, stands in the line talking to a man wearing a Superman tee shirt. She is laughing, picking pieces from a stick of blue cotton candy, and popping them into her mouth. David always thinks it's strange to see schoolteachers in public, dressed in shorts and tee shirts, doing what regular people do. It just doesn't seem natural.

There's a slight jolt, and the Ferris Wheel starts moving again. The sun is bright, and the warm summer air whips through his hair as the ride reaches full speed. A breeze moves across the field, carrying the smell of corn dogs and musty canvas into the sky. The mechanical Frankenstein on top of the Spook House snarls and raises his arms as the neon green lights along the roof sizzle. *What a great day,* David thinks. He wants to scream "Yahoo" or "Yeehaw" at the top of his lungs, but he knows that would be stupid, so he just smiles and looks into the bright blue sky.

David checks his watch. It's four twenty-five. Down below, Lester is busy handing cigarettes to a group of teenage girls gathered around him. They giggle and dance as he lights their smokes one by one. Lester is lost in the moment.

Looking to his right again, David sees Herbie walking up the alley, kicking a can in front of him as he goes. Herbie's yellow tomcat, John Boy, follows him for a few steps before thinking better of it, flopping down in the alley, and scratching his back on the gray asphalt.

As David's car skims across the platform, he yells to Lester to let him off. Lester, though, is working hard to keep the girls' attention and doesn't hear him. The Ferris Wheel continues to turn, and David leans out of the car, waives his arms, and yells, "Hey, Herbie," at the top of his lungs. Herbie stops six feet from the edge of the street and scans the area. Donnie Kessler pulls up next to him on his bike. The two boys talk and laugh, then Donnie rides away.

David yells, "Herbie, I'm up here!" This time Herbie sees him, and he grins and waves. It's four twenty-seven.

Cecil Parsons is hurrying up North Street to deliver a large deluxe and a six-pack of Pepsi to the Smiths on Sixth. A group of teenage girls dancing under the Ferris Wheel in shorts and halter tops distracts him for just a second. He later tells the police, "That boy just came runnin' outta nowhere. There wasn't nothin' I could do."

David watches in horror as Herbie steps into the street and the white Plymouth smashes into him at forty-nine miles per hour (the police report will say twenty to twenty - five). He grips the safety bar with both hands. His heart races, and he breaks out in a cold sweat.

Herbie's pelvis is crushed on impact, and his left femur is snapped in two. In an instant, he spins forty-five degrees, bends at the waist, and slams into the car's hood, shattering his face, tearing his aorta (the injury that takes Herbie's life), and severing his spinal cord between the C3 and C4 vertebrae. Herbie launches over the Plymouth eighteen feet in the air. He seems to hover for a few seconds, and it makes David think of when Herbie's mom took them to Pike Lake last summer, and they were doing cannonballs off the pier and into the water. A purple Chuck Taylor gym shoe lands right-side up on the car's roof next to the Furio's Pizza sign.

Herbie slams into the asphalt postmortem, breaking his right shoulder and three fingers on his left hand. He lies in the middle of the street with his face towards the Ferris Wheel and his arms and legs splayed at unnatural angles. His eyes are half open, and blood pours from his head and mouth.

A crowd moves toward the street. Donnie Kesler, the white-haired woman in the red apron, Elmo Gotlieb, and others form a semicircle and look at one another as if to say, *Somebody should do something.*

The Ferris Wheel continues to turn. Over and over, it turns.

Lester walks toward Herbie's broken body but stops at the edge of the street and vomits his still-cool lemonade onto the ground. The smoking girls huddle together, crying and puffing furiously on their cigarettes.

A policeman standing near the Spook House runs to Herbie and kneels beside him. David watches him remove his hat and make the sign of the cross.

There are sirens in the distance. An ambulance arrives, and two men dressed in white join the policeman kneeling next to Herbie. After a couple of minutes, one of the men goes to the ambulance and brings back a white sheet that he lays over Herbie. Blood soaks through and stains the sheet.

David closes his eyes tightly and then opens them wide, half expecting to awaken from a nightmare. To his great disappointment, though, his nightmare is real.

A feeling of doom comes over David, and he vomits over the side of the moving ride before losing control of his bladder. The warm wetness running down his legs is strangely comforting. "Get up, Herbie," he whispers.

David sees Herbie's mom running barefoot up the alley. The policeman stops her. She screams,

"Noooooooooo! My Herbie! Oh God, no!" Before collapsing on the street. The white-haired woman with the red apron kneels down by her and holds her as she sobs.

Donnie Kessler pedals away on his bike, and Emo Gotlieb drops his burlap bag and stretches his arms toward the sky in an appeal to God. David notices the numbers tattooed on the old man's left forearm. He's seen them before, 189734.

The Ferris wheel continues to turn on its axis, and David hears the sounds of Three Dog Night singing "Shambala." He starts to sing along.

The two men dressed in white place Herbie on a gurney and wheel it into the back of the ambulance. David covers his ears as Herbie's mother screams hysterically while being placed into the back seat of a police cruiser. The white-haired woman with the red apron climbs into the cruiser with her, and both vehicles slowly pull away. No lights, no sirens, no sense of urgency. It seems like it's not really an emergency at all.

Two cops and a man in a big hat continue talking to the pizza delivery driver, leaning against the back of his car, running his hands through his hair over and over again.

David watches a fire truck pull up. A man in rubber boots says something to the cops and then pours a jug of liquid on the large red spot in the road. He scrubs it with a push broom and then sprays it with water. The pink stream of suds makes its way toward the gutter and disappears under the street.

The two cops and the man in the big hat shake hands with the pizza delivery guy and slap him on his back as he gets into his car and drives away. It crosses David's mind that the pizza is probably cold by now.

Silently, David continues to ride the Ferris Wheel. He checks his watch. It's twelve minutes past five. He feels like he should cry, but the tears won't come. Instead, he thinks of the time he convinced Herbie to call Miss Buddwalk "Miss Ballsuck," and he laughs out loud.

The ride finally stops with David suspended ten feet in the air. Lester sits in a lawn chair, elbows on his knees, staring at the ground.

"Mister. I need to get off of here."

"Oh, I'm sorry, dude. I forgot you were there."

Lester lowers David to the ground and lets him off.

"Did you know him?" Lester asks, gesturing towards the wet spot in the street.

"His name's Herbie. We used to be friends."

A somber mood is in the air as David walks across the field. The Gorilla Girl stands outside her tent smoking a cigarette and looks away when David makes eye contact. The rides sit silent. Many people have gone home, but others stand huddled in small groups talking in hushed tones. Some people stare at David as he walks past. Others nod or point subtly as if to say, "Look, it's the dead boy's friend."

David stops and buys a candy apple. He stares at it for a long minute and thinks how the shiny red glaze on the apple reminds him of blood soaking through a white sheet. He drops the apple onto the ground and walks on.

When he gets to the ring toss game, David stops and gives the man behind the counter fifty cents. The man hands him three plastic rings and says, "I think it's your lucky day, kid."

David eyes the wooden crate of pop bottles on the table eight feet away. He tosses a ring in a high arching trajectory toward the bottles. It bounces off two bottles, then goes around one near the center of the crate.

"We have a winner!" the man says, talking around the cigar clenched tightly in his teeth. "I told you it's your lucky day."

"I want that one," David says, pointing at the small mirrors hanging on a post.

"Which one? The one with the marijuana leaf?"

"No, the one with the half-naked girl."

The man hands David the mirror and let's go with a blast of cigar smoke that seems to get stuck in the sticky air. David takes the mirror and walks away.

Passing the Merry-Go-Round, David doesn't see Marilyn Trainor sitting alone, robbed of her moment, and looking dejected. Nor does he notice the fire department's fish sandwich stand, which has no line for the first time in maybe forever.

Without realizing it, David heads for home. Donnie Kessler rides past him on his bike. He is standing up on his pedals and blowing a big pink bubble. The boys don't speak. After all, what is there to say?

As he walks up the sidewalk towards his house, David makes no effort to avoid the cracks, and he pays no mind to Mrs. Adams across the street, who looks up from her roses for a moment and waives.

His parents are sitting on the couch watching the evening news when David walks through the door.

"You're home early. We heard sirens a little bit ago. Did something happen at the carnival?" his father says, not taking his eyes off the television.

"Where's Herbie? Isn't he spending the night?" his mother asks.

David starts toward the stairs, then stops and hands his mother the prize mirror. "No. We're not friends anymore."

THE CARNIVAL 2

Ten-year-old Herbie Farmer sits on the front steps of his house at 721 Lafayette Street while John Boy, his big yellow tomcat, lies napping at his feet. Speckled rays of sunshine sneak through the leaves of the tall maple trees lining the street and dance around them.

Herbie's eight-year-old sister, Megan, is skipping rope on the sidewalk and singing, "Herbie and David sitting in a tree; K-I-S-S-I-N-G. First came love, then came marriage, then came Herbie with a turd in a carriage. 1-2-3-4-5!"

Herbie tells her to shut up and slings a rock in her direction as their mom pulls into the driveway from work.

"Mommy!" Megan squeals.

Fiona Farmer gets out of her car with three bags of groceries in her arms and her car keys dangling from one finger.

"Mommy, guess what," Megan says with excitement in her voice. "Herbie threw a rock at me."

"He did?" Fiona answers. "I wonder why he would do a thing like that?"

"I don't know. Maybe he just hates me."

"Maybe you just pester him to death sometimes, huh?"

Megan sighs. "Maybe."

"Herbie, don't throw rocks at your sister."

Herbie grins.

"There. Problem solved. Now, help me get these groceries in."

Herbie and Megan each take a bag and walk inside the house with their mother.

"Don't forget, Mom," Herbie says. "I'm going to the carnival and spending the night at David's house."

"Mommy! Why does Herbie get to go to the carnival? I wanna go!" Megan whines.

"For crying out loud, Megan, you know darn good and well that I'm taking you and Lori tomorrow evening. Now, cut the drama before I change our plans.".

"Fine then," Megan says with an air of dejection and walks up the steps to her room.

Turning back to Herbie, Fiona says, "I didn't forget. What time are you leaving?"

"Right now. It's almost four twenty - five, and I'm meeting David at the Ferris Wheel at four-thirty."

"How much money do you have, sweetie?"

"Six dollars."

Fiona walks into the kitchen and takes the Hill's Brothers coffee can that she keeps her tips in from the cabinet over the stove. "Here you go," she says, handing Herbie a wrinkled five-dollar bill.

Herbie looks at his mother. "It's OK, mom. Six dollars is plenty."

"Maybe if it was 1920," Fiona says with a smile. "Take it and have a good time. Ride as many rides as you can ride and eat as much carnival food as you can eat."

"Thanks, Mom," Herbie replies, feeling a vague sense

of guilt and embarrassment over the transaction.

"You'd better git, Mister. I'll swing past David's house later and drop off your toothbrush and pajamas."

"OK. See ya later, Mom."

"Bye, baby. Have fun."

Herbie walks out the back door, across the yard, and through the side gate to the alley that leads one block to the practice field.

"And be good at David's house!" Fiona yells through the open kitchen window.

"I will!" Herbie promises as he starts up the alley, kicking an empty Mountain Dew can before him. John Boy follows for a few steps before flopping down to scratch his back on the asphalt.

Herbie can hear the happy sounds of the carnival as they drift down the alley on the fried food-scented breeze blowing lightly toward him. He laughs, thinking about last year's carnival and how he chickened out of going into the Spook House at the last minute. David got mad and called him a "nerd" and a "crying ass pussy." They didn't speak for two days. He thinks of the rides and can't wait to get on the Scat and the Swings. He thinks of caramel apples, cotton candy, lemonade, and fried fish sandwiches. He thinks of winning a zippo lighter from the guy with hooks for hands that runs the quarter-pusher game. He thinks of spending the night at David's house, pizza from Furio's, watching Fritz the Night Owl, and having Mrs. Tuttle's pancakes for breakfast.

Up ahead, Herbie sees Mrs. Harris poking around with a stick in her burning trash can. She is known around the neighborhood as having a particular affinity for stirring her trash while it burns. No one knows why, but it seems to be her only pleasure in life.

Herbie checks his watch. It's four twenty - six.

As he approaches North Street, Herbie crushes the Mountain Dew can with his foot and notices Emo Gotlieb at the end of the alley talking to Harold Dixon, who is wearing a big dumb-looking hat. Emo is a bonafide Greenfield legend. He speaks with a heavy Polish accent and is Greenfield's only Holocaust survivor. The numbers tattooed on his forearm, 189734, are kept covered with his sleeve, but he doesn't mind showing them to anyone who asks. Especially kids. Herbie has always been in awe of Emo in a freakshow three-legged man kind of way. Harold owns Dixon's Grocery, and Herbie sees him sometimes when he goes shopping with his mother. There is something about Harold that doesn't sit right with Herbie. Perhaps it's the big ring on his pinky finger. Maybe it's because he smells so spicy from all the aftershave he wears. Or it could be how he talks to his mother with his hand on her shoulder. All the time with that big toothy smile. "Darlin" this and "Sweetheart" that. Herbie thinks it's creepy.

Reaching the end of the alley, Herbie stands, looking across the street at the carnival spread out before him. He thinks for a second that he hears someone call his name and scans the area around the Ferris Wheel, looking for David.

Donnie Kessler rides up on his bike and tells Herbie that Jack Connor got sick on the Tilt-a-Whirl and threw up on himself and Paula Delaney. They both laugh, then Donnie pedals away.

Herbie pauses at the edge of the street and, oddly, thinks of his mother and how tired she looks after coming home from waiting tables all day. For a brief but distinct moment, he is overcome with sorrow.

"Herbie! I'm up here!"

Herbie looks up and sees David laughing and waving

from atop the Ferris Wheel as it turns over and over. Herbie grins and waves back. It's four twenty - seven.

As he steps onto North Street, Herbie Farmer doesn't see the white Plymouth Duster with the Furio's Pizza sign on the roof and Cecil Parsons behind the wheel. All he sees is a bright flash. All he feels is a warm rush. All he thinks is how happy he is to be here.

(FROM GREENFIELD, OHIO) THE LOVE BROTHERS!

The locker room was hot, and the smell of sweaty socks and disinfectant hanging in the air made me nauseous. On top of that, my new mask was a half size too small and it squeezed my temples enough to give me a headache. I ate a couple Tums for my stomach and chased them with two Tylenol for my aching head. Then I rinsed my mouth with Gatorade and spit in the sink.

Looking in the mirror, I could see Buddy pacing behind me. His boots clicked and clacked with every step on the sticky floor. "You ready, man?" I asked.

"Hell yeah. I'm ready, brother."

The door opened, and a faceless voice called out, "Five minutes, guys."

I could hear the sound of the crowd picking up. Scattered booing at first. Then it became a chorus. That meant the bad guys were in the ring. Or were they the good guys? It was hard to tell in 1984 because Buddy and I had blurred the lines over the previous two years.

The door opened again, and Joe Squiers walked in.

31

"Looking good, Joe," Buddy said, continuing to pace.

"Christ, it's two hundred degrees in here," Joe answered, wiping his brow with a Dairy Queen napkin.

At sixty-eight years old, Joe Squiers still cut an imposing figure. A little over six feet tall and standing ramrod straight, his shaved head, handlebar mustache, and double-breasted black suit with a red handkerchief made him look like he should be on a can of pipe tobacco. He wore cordovan wingtips and carried a mahogany walking stick with a faux diamond handle for effect.

"One minute," the faceless voice called from the hallway.

"Boys," Joe said. "It's time to go to work."

"Ladies and gentlemen. This next match is the main event of the evening. One fall, with a sixty-minute time limit."

We walked down the hallway and stopped just short of the curtain. The crowd was buzzing. My stomach was in knots. Buddy was marching in place. Joe fiddled with his tie.

"For the GWA World Tag Team Championship. Introducing first, the challengers...,"

The crowd let go with another chorus of boos.

"... from El Segundo, California. Standing six feet nine inches tall and weighing in at three hundred and twenty pounds, ..."

"Damn, he's a big son of a bitch," Buddy whispered.

"... the former United States Heavyweight Champion, Big Dick Richards! Richards."

"Damn, here it comes!" I lifted my mask and puked a gallon of water into the trash can next to Joe, who never flinched.

"His partner, weighing in at two hundred fifty-five pounds. The meanest man in professional wrestling. From Granite City, Illinois. Dirty Dan Carson! Carson."

The crowd hissed and booed.

Suddenly, the opening guitar riff of The Rolling Stones' "Tumbling Dice" blasted out over the public address system.

We burst through the curtain, and the place went crazy. The roar was deafening. Hands reached out to touch us as the security guards pushed back the crowd.

"Their opponents. Making their way to the ring...,"

The nerves were gone. We reveled in the adulation.

"... accompanied by their manager, Gentleman Joe Squiers."

Out of the corner of my eye, I saw something coming toward me, and I caught a pink bra right before it hit me in the face. "Bobby, Bobby!" I turned to my left and saw a beautiful blonde lift her shirt and blow me a kiss."

A couple feet away, Buddy was fighting off a short middle-aged redhead who was grabbing at his crotch.

Joe grinned like a hungry fox running free in a henhouse.

"They are the reigning GWA Tag Team Champions of The World!"

Mick and the Stones were belting out "Tumbling Dice" as we neared the ring. A man wearing an "I Love Big Dick" tee shirt stepped out from the crowd and pointed his finger at Joe, who promptly whacked him across the head with his walking stick. The man went down, and the cops hauled him away.

"At a combined weight of five hundred thirty - five pounds. From Greenfield, Ohio...,"

We finally made it to the ring and stepped through the ropes. Richards and Carson were scowling as Buddy and I took the championship belts from around our waists and held them high over our heads. Joe walked up and down the ring apron, whipping the crowd into a frenzy.

"Buddy. Bobby. The Love Brothers! Love Brothers."

We handed the belts to the referee, who showed them first to Richards and Carson, then to the crowd before passing them to a ring attendant.

(Lance Russell) "Hello, again everybody. Lance Russell and Dave Brown right along ringside and we're about ready to go! This one is gonna be a doozy!"

(Dave Brown) "It sure is, Lance. Buddy and Bobby Love defending the world tag team titles in their hometown against the number one contenders, Big Dick Richards and Dirty Dan Carson."

(Lance Russell) "You know, it was two years ago tonight that Buddy and Bobby won the titles from Tank Kizer and Slim Myers in a wild brawl down in Wheeling, West Virginia."

(Dave Brown) "People still talk about that one, and I think this one here tonight will be just as memorable."

(Lance Russel) "Without a doubt. These two teams have battled all across the country and they do not like each other, Dave. Dick Richards is looking for revenge because two weeks ago, in Dayton, Buddy and Bobby caught him in the locker room alone, and they whipped him like a dirty yard dog. Then, to add insult to injury, they shaved off his eyebrows and left him lying in a toilet stall. But hey, that's the way the Love Brothers operate. You find yourself on their bad side, and they'll chop you down to size no matter how big you are. They are two rugged individuals and they'll feed you some knuckles right now. Then they'll humiliate you on top of it. They do not mess around."

(Dave Brown) There are several celebrities on hand here tonight at the Greenfield Meadowlands. GWA President Howard Burnett is here of course. Former Ohio State quarterback Art Schlichter stopped to say hello a moment ago. Actress Traci Lords is here with a large entourage. Country music star Johnny Paycheck is sitting right behind us, and twelve-time Southern Ohio Heavyweight champion King Sheik is lurking about as well. King is retired now, of course, and owns a barber shop in Greenfield, we hear."

(Lance Russell) *"That's some real star power, Dave. It sounds like maybe we'd better get our autograph books ready."*

(Dave Brown) *"The Love Brothers are wearing long black tights with their first names down the right leg, white boots, and their distinctive black and white masks. Across the ring, Dick Richards is sporting red trunks with "Big Dick" emblazoned on the back and black boots. Dan Carson is wearing a white singlet and red boots."*

We walked to the center of the ring and got our instructions from the referee. No closed fists, no hair pulling, clean breaks when instructed, and so forth. All the standard stuff. Carson smelled like he'd been sucking on a clove of garlic, and Big Dick was sweating and gritting his teeth. I burst out laughing when I saw the two white patches where Dick's eyebrows used to be.

When we returned to our corner, Joe told Buddy to start the match and "Run 'em to death." Buddy was the high flier, you see. Whipping around the ring, landing drop kicks, and flying off the ropes. I was the brawler. Pile drivers, body slams, and suplexes were my specialties. Buddy would wear 'em out, and I'd finish 'em off.

(Lance Russell) *"Alright, we're about to get this one underway as referee Jerry Calhoun sends both teams to their corners. I gotta tell you, Dave, the Love Brothers look about as good tonight as I've ever seen them. Buddy doesn't have an ounce of fat on him, and Bobby looks to have bulked up a little in the upper body. His arms are massive."*

(Dave Brown) *"You're right, Lance. They are looking good for this partisan crowd here at the Meadowlands."*

(Lance Russell) *"There's the bell. It'll be Dan Carson and The L Train, Buddy Love, starting the match for their respective teams."*

The bell rang, and Buddy went to work on Dirty Dan. He cycled through a series of arm bars and headlocks, then used a snap mare to take Carson to the canvas. A kick to the side of Dan's head got his bells ringing, then Buddy whipped him into the ropes and landed a perfect dropkick on the rebound. Big Dick tried to get into the ring, but the referee pushed him back through the ropes. Buddy tagged me in, and I gave Carson a couple kicks to the ribs, then dropped a knee to his face. I grabbed Dan by the hair and pulled him to his feet and noticed blood trickling from his right nostril. As I started scooping him up for a body slam, Carson slipped away and tried to get behind me for a full nelson, but I shook him off and caught him with a jab that opened a gash over his left eye. I ran him headfirst into a turnbuckle, then tagged Buddy back in. Buddy applied a headlock, but Carson slipped out and landed a haymaker to the side of Buddy's head, dropping him to the canvas. Dan tagged Richards, who stepped over the top rope and into the ring. I knew Buddy was about to get pounded by Big Dick, so I…

"Jack! Are you up? Jack Connor, get out of that bed! You're going to be late for school!"

I sat up and rubbed my eyes. For a moment, I couldn't figure out what was going on.

"Jack! JACK CONNOR!"

"Huh?"

"Are you up?"

"Holy shit, mom! Yes, I'm up!"

"Then get out of that bed!"

"Okay!"

"Donnie Kessler is waiting out front. He said to bring your mask. Something about giving his little brother a title shot after school or some nonsense like that."

Damn, what a dream, I thought. *The Love Brothers. The Greenfield Meadowlands. Lance Russel and Dave Brown.* That's some funny shit!

I pulled on a dirty pair of jeans and a clean tee shirt, then grabbed my shoes from under the bed. I picked up the black and white mask lying on my dresser and shoved it into my back pocket.

Two months had gone by since Donnie and I bought cheap wrestling masks out of the back of a magazine. We had proclaimed ourselves world tag team champions and our guidance counselor, Mr. Squiers helped us print calling cards that made the claim seem legitimate. At least to us.

It was my idea to start driving around Greenfield with our masks on and pulling over to give title shots to unsuspecting opponents wherever we saw them, in their front yards, in the center of town, walking home from school, it didn't matter. Our opponents were usually unsuspecting underclassmen or our little brothers and their friends. We took on all comers like real champions should. Donnie and I were undefeated in these impromptu matches.

My mom gave me an unapproving look as I ran down the steps then strutted out the front door and hopped into Donnie's '75 Chevelle.

"Bobby Love!" Donnie said with a grin.

"Buddy Love!" I answered. "Let's defend the belts."

"WOOOOOO!" Donnie proclaimed as we sped up Second Street towards school.

The sun was shining, the windows were down, and the Stones were on the radio. Life couldn't possibly be any better than it was just then.

Hell yes! From Greenfield, Ohio, The Love Brothers!

FIONA

PART ONE

Fiona Farmer lay on her back and studied the ceiling. The light fixture over the bed was missing its shade, and the single glowing bulb cast a weird shadow that turned the stain around the light into a piece of art vaguely resembling Van Gogh's "Dream Tree."

"Here it comes. Give me the claws!" The sweaty man on top of her was searching for glory, and Fiona dug her long red nails into his fat hairy back as he shot off into the promised land. His eyes rolled back in his head as he called out to God, "Good Lord! Yes!" He grunted, grunted again, and moaned before rolling off Fiona and onto the mattress beside her.

Fiona wiped Harold Dixon's sweat from her face with the sheet, then got out of bed. She walked to the window and parted the curtains just enough to peek out at the motel parking lot. It was drizzling rain, and the streetlights reflected off the wet blacktop. A large brown dog wandered across the lot, stopped to sniff a crumpled

Kentucky Fried Chicken bag lying on the ground, then hiked his leg and peed on the bumper of the green station wagon parked outside the door. Across the lot, Fiona watched a thin man in a suit fumbling with his room key, trying to unlock the door. He had a briefcase in his left hand and wore glasses with oversized plastic frames. A large worn suitcase sat on the sidewalk behind him. After opening his door, the thin man turned his head towards Fiona, peeking from behind the curtain. They briefly made eye contact before he picked up his suitcase and ducked into his room. Fiona thought, *he doesn't look like the kind of man that would pay a woman for sex.*

"Bring me a cigarette, will you, Fiona?"

Fiona closed the curtain, picked up the pack of Winstons from the table, lit two, and gave one to the sweating man lying in bed. Then she went into the bathroom and turned the water on in the sink.

"How was it?" Harold asked.

"How was what?" Fiona replied over the running water.

"Gotdammit, you know what. How was it? Did I make you… you know."

"What difference does that make, Harold? Worry about making your wife… you know, not me. My job is to make YOU… you know."

Harold sat up on the edge of the bed. "Ahh, fuck it," he said.

Fiona flushed the toilet and walked back into the room. "Your back's a mess. Better keep your shirt on when you get home."

Harold picked up his wallet and car keys from the nightstand and walked into the bathroom, locking the door behind him. Fiona heard the shower come on, and Harold started singing, "*I come to the garden duh duh, while the dew is still on the roses, duh duh duh duh, do do duh duh. The duh duh duh discloses. And he walks with me, and he talks duh duh. And he tells me do duh duh duh."*

Harold turned off the water, walked out of the bathroom, and got dressed.

Fiona, still naked, (Harold didn't like her getting dressed before he left), sat on the bed waiting.

"Well?" Harold said as he pulled five twenty-dollar bills out of his wallet.

Fiona looked at him without moving.

"Get over here."

Fiona got up and walked over to where Harold was standing. Harold looked at her, and she looked down at her feet.

"You're going to have to get over it, Fiona," Harold announced, waving his hands in the air. "You go through the same shit this time every year. It's been ten years. Get on with your life."

Fiona continued to look at her feet. "Can you just pay me, please?"

"Hmph. You're not worth what Jerry's charging these days. You don't put any effort into it anymore. You're a whore, for crying out loud. Start acting like one. Take a little pride in your work."

"I'm not a whore."

"Oh, yeah. If there was ever a living, breathing whore on this Earth, Fiona, it's you."

"Fuck you, Harold!"

Harold gave Fiona's cheek a sharp slap, and she felt the tears welling up in her eyes.

"A smart-mouthed whore to boot," Harold said, pointing his finger in Fiona's face. "Jerry should take that shit out of you. He's too easy on you whores."

Fiona said nothing.

"Stop stalling. You're gonna make me miss the beginning of St. Elsewhere."

Fiona sighed and got down on her knees in front of Harold. She looked up at him with big wet eyes as he let the fistful of twenty-dollar bills rain down on her face. It was the way he always paid. It kept things in the proper order. For him, it kept up the wall of separation. After all, he was a respected pillar of the community. For her, it was customer satisfaction. Men like Harold get off on hurting women like Fiona, and she was still on the clock.

Harold walked to the door, opened it to leave, then turned back to Fiona. "Stop by the store this week. Lots of good sales. Ground chuck's just ninety-nine cents a pound. And Downy fabric softener is buy one get one free with a coupon."

"Yeah. Sounds.... amazing."

"You gotta have the coupon," Harold said, jabbing his finger into the air to emphasize the point.

"Got it," Fiona replied.

"I'll be in touch. Give Jerry my regards."

Fiona stared out the open door, past Harold, and focused on the big brown dog standing by his station wagon.

When he left, Fiona stood up, put the money in her purse, walked back to the window, and threw the curtains open wide. She watched Harold pull from the Lanes Motel parking lot onto Jefferson Street, and silently prayed that a semi would come over the hill and wipe him out. But no semi appeared, and Harold drove off into the night. Back to his big house on Hillcrest Drive with the swimming pool, hot tub, and tennis court. Back to his waiting wife. He would eat the dinner she had kept warm in the oven. They would have a glass of wine while he told her about his hard day at work. Then they would watch St. Elsewhere. When they went to bed, Harold would explain to his wife that he was, *"Just too tired for sex tonight."*

Turning around, Fiona looked around at the ugly room, bathed in light from the streetlamp outside. The stain in the center of the ceiling no longer looked like a work of art. Now, it looked like a piss-yellow water stain tinged with a dark brown outline.

Fiona closed the curtains. She stood naked in the middle of the room and felt the crusty carpet beneath her feet. She closed her eyes, stood on her toes, stretched her arms out wide, and imagined floating away to someplace new. Someplace void of the memories and the reminders. Someplace without Harold Dixon. Someplace different than this.

Before falling deep into her emotions, Fiona took the pint of Jim Beam from her purse and poured a double into the glass on the bathroom sink. She swirled it around and drank it down in one motion. Then she wrapped herself in the extra blanket from the closet and fell asleep on the bed she had just used to pay her electric bill.

Fiona jerked herself awake and felt the paralysis leave her body. The figure in the corner was gone. Was he ever really there? He came nearly every night and stared at her. Sometimes he came close to the bed and stared at her. His face was not defined, and his limbs were bent at right angles. She tried to talk to him but couldn't. She tried to look away but couldn't. She was vulnerable. And naked of course. It was always the same.

The alarm clock said two twenty-one a.m. Fiona lit a cigarette and stared into the darkness. Some people hate the night. Not Fiona. She considered the night to be her refuge. A person can be themselves in the dark. Fiona would have been just as happy if the sun never shone again.

The odor of mildew drifting from the bathroom and the lingering scent of Harold's Aqua Velva was a familiar smell. Fiona had entertained hundreds of men (and a handful of women) over the past nine years. Most of them in dingy motel rooms like this all-over southern Ohio. White men, black men, young men, old men, tall men, short men, rich men, poor men, good men, bad men, married men, single men, men with power, and men with none. Lawyers, doctors, preachers, teachers, plumbers, barbers, cops, small-town mayors, traveling businessmen, and more eighteen-year-old boys stepping into manhood than she cared to remember. Most were friendly enough. A few even professed their love for her and talked of marriage. A handful took pleasure in inflicting physical pain on her. Fiona had learned to deal with that and simply charged a fee for their indulgence. Only one humiliated her, though, and made her feel like the person she had become.

Harold Dixon was a big deal in Greenfield. He was fifty-nine years old, and his list of small-town accomplishments was a mile long:

Highland County's Baby New Year in 1927.

First Team All SCOL quarterback in 1943 and 1944.

Salutatorian of the McClain High School Class of 1945.

Two years on occupation duty with the U.S. Army in Japan in 1946 and 1947.

Graduated from Ohio University with a degree in business in 1952.

Opened Dixon's Grocery on South Street in 1954.

Married former Miss Southern Ohio, Darlene Dietrich, in 1955.

Elected to the Greenfield Exempted Village School

Board in 1958.

Celebrated the birth of his son, Edward, in 1959.

Moved his grocery store to a big new building on Jefferson Street in 1961.

Expanded his store in 1963 and again in 1965.

Ordained a Deacon at Cornerstone Baptist Church in 1966.

Celebrated the birth of his daughter, Elizabeth, in 1967.

Became a Master Mason in 1969.

Expanded his store again in 1971.

Named an Elector to the Democratic National Convention in 1972.

Became a Scottish Rite Mason in 1974.

Elected President of the Tiger Boosters, voted Greenfield's Man of the Year, and named Grand Marshal of Greenfield's Bicentennial Parade all in 1976.

Appointed to fill a vacancy on the Greenfield city council in 1981.

Named Chairman of the Highland County Chamber of Commerce Board of Directors in 1984.

Although not part of his official record of accomplishments, it should be noted that Harold Dixon started visiting Jerry Garner's stable of harlots shortly after Jerry opened his side business in 1973. According to Jerry's detailed records, between 1977 and 1986, Harold had seen Fiona Farmer eighty-one times.

Fiona snuffed out her cigarette in the ashtray and dozed off again. She dreamt of a family with a house and a cat. She dreamt of sunshine and laughter and happiness. She dreamt of Ferris Wheels and cotton candy. She dreamt of blood and sorrow and darkness. She cried. Or perhaps she dreamt she cried.

At six-fifteen a.m., a car pulled up outside Room 108

of the Lanes Motel, and Fiona got inside. Mike Lipps, Jerry's driver, enforcer, debt collector, and gopher, handed Fiona a Styrofoam cup of coffee and quickly pulled out of the parking lot and onto Jefferson Street. "Good morning, sunshine. How was your evening?" he asked without taking his eyes off the road.

"Oh, it was like a dream. Harold Dixon swept me off my feet," Fiona responded.

"I bet it was. I'd put my foot up his fat ass if Jerry let me."

"I'd pay to watch it," Fiona said while pulling back the tab on the coffee lid and taking a sip. "Years ago, whenever I would go into his store, back before things got like they are now, he would put his hands all over me. He really gave me the creeps. Always asking me out. Even offered me money a few times. I almost did it once because I needed new tires on my car. He's never mentioned any of it, though. It's like it never happened. I think he's paying me back for all the rejection I dumped on his head."

"I'll get a crack at him one day. You wait and see," Mike said as he pulled up in front of Fiona's apartment over top of the Diamond Grill.

Fiona took a wad of cash out of her purse and handed it to Mike, who counted out one hundred dollars.

Mike placed the five twenty-dollar bills into a blue People's National Bank bag and handed Fiona a fifty-dollar bill in exchange.

"Tip?" Mike asked.

"From Harold Dixon? Are you kidding me?"

Mike looked at Fiona without speaking.

"No, Mike. No tip."

"OK. You know what'll happen if Jerry finds out he ain't getting a taste of your tips, right?

Fiona knew precisely what would happen. Jerry wouldn't lay a hand on his girls, but he'd tell Mike to, and Mike would do it. Not because he wanted to, or because he enjoyed it, but because he worked for Jerry, and it was a part of his job.

"Jerry gets twenty percent of tips now. You know that. He might ease up on that eventually, but the economy is shit right now, and the business is in a crisis. You know. Reaganomics. White folks is hurtin' these days. It makes sense, right?"

"Makes perfect sense," Fiona answered somewhat sarcastically.

Not only would Jerry have Mike use the back of his hand to make his point, but he'd also put the girls on probation for infractions. Cheating Jerry out of money meant no work for sixty days. No questions asked. Withholding favors from Jerry or talking about the business in public would get a girl at least thirty days. Belligerence, talking back, or acting snotty towards Jerry was a week to ten days, depending on who the girl was. Client complaints about laziness, rudeness, timeliness, or cleanliness meant three to five days, depending on the client's importance. During probation, Jerry wouldn't put a girl on the schedule at all, and he would make them work the midnight to eight shift at the textile factory for half pay with no days off. He was tough and not always fair, but he was better than most small-town pimps. Jerry had guys like Harold Dixon, who carried a lot of clout around Greenfield, in his back pocket, and they made sure the mayor's office and the police department turned a blind eye to his textile plant brothel.

"You're on again tonight. Back at The Lanes. Room 101. One hour. I'll pick you up at eight-thirty. The client will be there at nine o'clock. One hour. Not a minute more. I'll park across the lot, so I can see the door. Jerry doesn't trust this guy, and he doesn't want you to spend the night in the room."

"Who's the client?"

"Some hilljack from Bourneville. Young guy. He dug some post holes for Jerry or some shit like that. He's kinda slow. Jerry felt sorry for him and decided to hook him up."

"Are you kidding me? A charity fuck? I've worked for Jerry nine freakin' years, and I'm getting pimped out to a toothless fuckbilly from Bainbridge for a charity fuck?"

"Bourneville."

Fiona looked at Mike. "What?"

"The toothless fuckbilly. He's from Bourneville. Not Bainbridge."

"It's the same thing, Mike! A welfare fuck for some inbred Ross County redneck."

"Damn, girl! You ain't working for free. You'll get paid. I'll have an Andy Jackson waiting in the car when you come out."

Fiona shook her head. "Why can't one of the new girls do it? That chubby blonde or the Asian chick from Washington Court House. I'm getting shitty assignments these days. No out of towners, no parties, no VIPs. I used to get those. What gives, Mike?"

"For starters, you ain't the only three holer anymore. Bonnie Bishop opened the back door for business five weeks ago and she's getting ten percent more dates than before.

"That's one extra date a week, Mike. Don't blow smoke."

"Look, my black ass don't do the scheduling. Jerry does. So, I'm just making an educated guess, OK?"

Fiona looked blankly at Mike and sipped her coffee.

"You're thirty-five years old. You been at this for nine years, and guys like change. Plus, you don't take care of yourself like you used to. And the booze. Holy shit, Fiona."

"I see. I'm trash now."

"I didn't say you was trash. You ain't trash. You just ain't in your prime no more. Guys are asking for the younger girls. Except for Harold. He never asks for anyone but you."

Fiona glared at Mike.

"Look. Get off the booze. Clean yourself up a little, and you have two or three decent years left. You could still get some prime assignments. Make as much money as you can and save it. Then you can retire and go to the plant and run a sewing machine, clean the bathrooms, or whatever. You know Jerry always finds a place for his girls. At least the ones who don't screw him over."

Fiona stared down Jefferson Street and waited for Mike to finish. "Thanks for the pep talk, Mike. I'll see you this evening."

Fiona got out of the car, slammed the door, and went up to her apartment. She needed a shower and a drink.

PART TWO

Fiona poured herself a rum and coke, then walked into the bathroom, turned on the shower, and looked in the mirror. The years looked back at her.

For the first few months after the accident, Fiona got by better than could be expected. She returned to work two days after the funeral and was holding it together pretty well for a while. She started coaching softball again and considered enrolling in paralegal classes at Southern State. The whole town had rallied around her. Cash donations, thoughts and prayers, cards, flowers, and casseroles poured in. She had more friends than she could count. Then everyone gradually got back to their own lives and left Fiona to hers.

On the first anniversary of the accident, Fiona woke up in her own vomit after eating a handful of pills and drinking a pint of whiskey. A few days later, she sent her daughter, Megan, off to live with her parents in Indiana and checked into a rehab facility in Athens. On the third day, she checked herself out and returned to Greenfield.

Fiona moved out of her house on Lafayette Street and into the apartment over the Diamond Grill. She continued working as a waitress at Tuck's Diner during the and started tending bar in the evenings. One night, Jerry Garner came in for a drink and offered her a job sewing at the Textile factory for six dollars an hour. Fiona accepted. Jerry moved her from the plant floor to the reception desk two months later. Within a few weeks, he added her to his stable, earning up to four hundred dollars a day.

Although she became a pariah to Greenfield's polite society, Fiona was a hit from day one with the men who moved around in the town's seedy underbelly of undercover gambling, beer joints, drug dealers, and illicit sex. She looked like she had stepped out of a magazine. Twenty-six years old, five foot four inches tall in heels, long dark hair, and beautiful green eyes. Plus, she was someone that everybody knew. Guys that had been hitting on her in vain at the cafe for three years could just call and schedule an appointment now.

Fiona studied her face in the mirror. The young

mother was gone. Heartache and alcohol were taking a toll on her. She wondered how long she could go on. "Stop feeling sorry for yourself, Fiona, you fucking ho. That ain't gonna fix a thing," she said out loud, then finished her drink.

Fiona spent the day taking naps, watching soap operas, smoking weed, and painting her nails. At seven thirty, she had a bite to eat, then took another quick shower, put on some basic makeup, and dressed in jeans and a tee shirt. No way was she getting all dolled up for a charity fuck with some inbred white trash knuckle dragger.

It was at eight twenty - seven, when Mike pulled up out front. In nine years, she had never known him to be one minute late. He was the only thing in her life that she could depend on. The thought made her both happy and sad as she headed downstairs for her date.

PART THREE

Fiona's charity date was over and she looked out through the peephole in the door waiting for Mike to pull the car up. When he did, she went outside and slipped quickly into the front seat.

"Everything OK?" Mike asked.

"Yeah. Poor hick sucked on my toes for thirty minutes and couldn't get it up. I felt a little sorry for him. We ended up just smoking a joint and talking."

"No shit?" Mike said. "Stage fright. They say it happens sometimes. It ain't never happened to me. But it does happen sometimes, I hear."

Fiona cracked her window and lit a cigarette.

"I've got some good news," Mike said.

"Yeah?" Fiona replied.

"You're going out of town for a couple days."

"Really? With who?"

"Harold Dixon."

"What? Why?"

"He's going to some meeting in Cincinnati and wants to take you along. You leave Wednesday morning and get back Friday night."

"What's the pay?"

"Four hundred plus meals."

"You know, Wednesday is ten years, Mike."

Mike nodded his head. "I knew it was coming up."

"I'm not sure I can do it. Too much to think about."

"Maybe a couple days out of town will help take your mind off things."

"You really think a couple days in Cincinnati with Harold Dixon will take my mind off anything, Mike?"

"Probably not," Mike said as he dropped Fiona off at her apartment. "Jerry's going to insist you go, though. Dixon won't want anybody else."

Fiona started to say something, then stopped.

"Here's your twenty bucks. Might be the easiest twenty you ever made. You don't even need to take a shower before bed. Just wash your feet."

Fiona took the money, and a tear ran down her cheek. "My life has run off on me, Mikey. I don't even know what I'm doing anymore."

Mike put this hand on Fiona's leg and patted it gently. "I understand what you're saying. Trust me. I do."

PART FOUR

The phone rang, and Fiona sat up in bed. The clock on the nightstand said eleven twenty-five a.m.

"Hello," Fiona said, still half asleep.

"It's me, Mike."

"It's my day off, Mike."

"I know. It's not about business. I need to talk to you. Take a ride with me. I'll pick you up in an hour."

Fiona let out a long sigh. "Dammit Mike. This better be good."

Fiona got dressed and waited outside. When Mike pulled up, she climbed into the car and he sped off.

"Where are we headed?" Fiona asked.

"Nowhere in particular."

"OK," Fiona shrugged.

"Jerry said you're going with Harold to Cincinnati."

"Shit. I figured he'd make me go."

"It'll be fine. It's a big payday. You said last week that you wanted to do more out-of-towners."

"I know. It's just the timing, not to mention the client. This year is tougher than most. Maybe it's because it's been ten years since I lost my Herbie. Isn't ten years supposed to be a milestone for major events?

"I think so."

Fiona cracked the window and lit a cigarette.

Mike looked at Fiona. "Harold called Jerry and complained about your attitude. Said you aren't performing up to par."

"Who gives a fuck?"

"Jerry's gonna put you on the bench for a couple days after Cincinnati."

"For crying out loud. Harold Dixon is a whiny ass baby, and Jerry Garner is an asshole."

Mike nodded in agreement. "You ain't wrong."

"I thought you said this ride, or whatever the hell we're doing, wasn't work-related. Why are we on Rapid Forge Road, driving through Bum Fuck Egypt? You gonna put a bullet in my brain and bury me in a field or something? If you are, get it over with."

"Always so damn dramatic. Let's drive over to Paint Creek Lake. I ain't been over there in who knows how long."

"Whatever."

The two drove in silence for twenty minutes before Mike pulled into the parking lot at Paint Creek Lake and turned off the engine.

Fiona lit another cigarette. Then she looked at Mike. "Now what? You want a blowjob or something? You're acting weird."

Mike turned to Fiona. "I'm gonna tell you something I'm not supposed to tell you. And if it gets back to Jerry that I told you, I'm a dead man. You understand?"

"What the hell?"

"I'm serious, Fiona."

"Okay. I'm listening."

Mike took a deep breath. "Harold Dixon was there when your boy was killed."

"What are you talking about?"

"He was there. Eight feet away when Cecil Parsons hit Herbie. He saw the whole thing."

"What? I don't believe that. He would have talked about it. All the time we've spent together. He would have told me."

"Would he? Why?" Mike asked.

Fiona looked at Mike. "Why wouldn't he? Just to make me feel shitty if nothing else. He likes doing that, you know."

"Fiona, why do you think Parsons walked away that day without any charges?"

"They said it was an accident. Herbie ran into the street. There was nothing Parsons could do."

Mike shook his head. "Yeah, right."

"What do you know, Mike?"

"What you said is true. Herbie ran into the street, and Cecil Parsons didn't hit him on purpose. But there's more to it than that."

"Like what?" Fiona asked.

Mike paused. "Do you know that Harold Dixon is Cecil Parsons' great uncle and that he was there when the cops interviewed Parsons at the scene?"

"What?"

"Yeah. He saw the accident, realized it was Cecil driving the car, and spent ten minutes with him before the cop even got there. And that ain't all. The cop that interviewed Cecil? His wife and son worked at Dixon's Grocery. In fact, they still do. Other witnesses that were there, like that old Jew, Emo, and several teenage girls standing around the Ferris Wheel, all said Parsons was doing almost fifty miles per hour when he hit Herbie. They also said that Parsons didn't touch the brakes until he made impact. The accident report said Parsons was going thirty miles per hour, and evidence showed *the driver applied his brakes but could not keep from striking the subject who had darted into the street.*"

"What about the coroner? He would have known better."

Mike shook his head. "The coroner was Harold's lodge buddy. Plus, he was headed to Florida on vacation the next day and wanted to get outta town. He never even came to the scene. Just popped by the funeral home the next day and signed the papers.

Fiona looked stunned. "I can't believe this. How do you know all of this, Mike?"

"Jerry talks, and I listen. He acts like I ain't even in the room most of the time. I know shit about every asshole in Greenfield. Things that would...."

"How long have you known, Mike?"

"I guess I've always known."

"You son of a bitch." Fiona buried her face in her hands. I thought you were my friend. I've always trusted you."

Mike shook his head and looked down at the steering wheel. "I'm sorry, Fiona. I'm... I'm sorry... It's just...."

"To hell with sorry! And to hell with you!" Fiona screamed and punched Mike in the face.

Mike put his hand to his bleeding lip. "I deserve that," Mike said.

"You're damn right you do, you bastard."

"I'm so sorry," Mike said again.

"It's like Herbie didn't matter. Why didn't you tell me this before?" Fiona pleaded.

"Jerry didn't want you to know. He was afraid that you'd confront Harold and things would get messy. He was worried that the business would be exposed to the point that city hall couldn't turn a blind eye anymore, and they'd shut him down."

Fiona, hands shaking, chain lit another cigarette, took a long drag and exhaled. "Why are you telling me now?"

Mike hesitated. "Do you know why I'm in Greenfield?"

Fiona shrugged. "Why is anyone in Greenfield? Cursed maybe? I've never really thought about it."

"Because when I got back from Vietnam in 1969, I got on a train in San Francisco and headed east. I was going to Philadelphia. That's where I'm from. But I only had enough money to get to Cincinnati. I was sittin' in the train station, wondering how I was going to get home when I saw a guy I knew from basic training walk past. His name was Crawford Blanton. Country boy from Hurricane, West Virginia. Nice guy. Anyway, I hollered at him, and we sat and talked for a while. He asked me when my train was leaving, and I told him about my predicament. He reached into his pocket and gave me all the money he had. Three dollars and seventy-two cents. That was enough for me to get to Greenfield and still have six cents left."

Fiona flicked her cigarette out the window.

"When I got off the train in Greenfield," Mike continued, "I thought about things and decided I shouldn't go back to Philly. I was AWOL from the Army, and I didn't want my momma to have to deal with that. So, I decided to just stay here. I didn't figure the Army would ever come lookin' for me in this shithole town. And so far, they haven't. I called my momma and told her I was getting transferred to Hawaii, and I'd be home for Christmas. I ain't never been to Philadelphia since."

"You've never gone to visit your mom?" Fiona asked.

"Nope. I was gonna go at some point. I called again a couple months after I got here. We talked, and Momma told me some Military Police had stopped by and said they were looking for me. I told her there must be some mistake and I'd take care of it. When I called again a few days later, my sister told me that Momma had died that morning. I didn't go home for the funeral because I knew the MPs would be there."

"Damn. What did you do?"

"I cried," Mike answered.

"And then what?"

"Nothing. I just went on day by day."

"Where'd you live? How'd you eat?" Fiona asked.

"I went out to Dixon's Grocery the day after I got here and got a job stocking shelves. He let me stay in that old shed behind the store until I got my first paycheck. Then I went and got a room at the Elliot Hotel."

"No shit?"

"Yeah. Dixon used to call me *"Boy."* He would pull me aside and ask if I had stolen anything from him lately. Told me not to be lookin' at the white women when they was shoppin. All kinds of shit like that."

"That sounds like Harold," Fiona replied.

"I couldn't do nothin' because I was afraid of getting in trouble with the police, and the Army finding out and coming to get me. Anyway, I worked for Harold for about a year, then went to the textile factory and got a forklift job. That's where I met Jerry. The rest is history, as they say."

"There's still one thing I don't understand. Why are you telling me this now?"

Mike looked at Fiona and shrugged. "I'm tired of seeing guys like Harold Dixon get away with shittin' on everybody. Look, I ain't no saint. I've done some nasty things in my life. But you know the difference between people like me and people like Harold Dixon and even Jerry Garner?"

"Not really."

"I ain't never hurt nobody that wasn't in the game. I ain't out beating up innocent people or selling drugs to school kids. I ain't breaking in nobody's house. I ain't attacking women on the street. Everybody I've ever hurt was playing this game we play, and they knew the rules. Hell, a lot of them was trying to hurt me too, and I just beat 'em to the punch."

Fiona listened closely.

"Harold Dixon, on the other hand. That motherfucker used his influence in town to cover up the facts about your little boy's death. Cecil Parsons got off without so much as a slap on the wrist. Now, what's he doing? Layin' around and livin' off welfare. Back when I worked for him, Harold knew I had no money, no place to live, and no family here. Yeah, he gave me a job. But he paid me thirty cents less than everyone else and treated me like shit because I'm black."

"I've never thought of it that way. You have a point. In a bizarre way, you have a point," Fiona said.

"Remember when Sam Wilson bought Super Value, and it caught fire right after he finished renovating it? Two days before the grand fucking reopening! That was Dixon. Sam Wilson ain't never bothered nobody. He's a decent guy. Harold just wanted to hurt him. I've seen that asshole re-label day-old meat and leave it on the shelf three days past expiration. He don't care. He don't eat the shit. I could go on and on."

Fiona took a deep breath and shook her head.

Mike started the car then banged his hands on the steering wheel. You know what I really hate, though? I hate the way he treats you. You don't deserve it."

The ride back to Greenfield was a quiet one.

As they crossed the bridge into Greenfield, Mike broke the silence. "Something bad is gonna happen to Harold Dixon. He plays the game. He knows the rules. He understands how dangerous things can be. Yeah, something bad is gonna happen."

"Mike. I play the game too. If I get hurt, I get hurt. I know the rules."

"It ain't the same. You don't play it because you want to. You just got pulled in. Jerry took advantage of you because you were hurting and needed something. He knew he could provide that something and make money off of you to boot."

Mike pulled the car into the King Quick lot and put it in Park.

"Fiona, I've heard you talk about Herbie, but you never talk about your daughter."

"Hmm. Megan. She's eighteen now. Just graduated from high school. She's in Tipton, Indiana, with my parents."

"Do you ever see her?"

"I've not seen her in over five years. I used to go visit her at Christmas and once or twice in the summer. The last time was in 1981. Megan told me not to come back. So, I didn't. I still write her letters. She never writes back."

"That's rough."

"I can almost forgive myself for letting Herbie go to the carnival that day. There was no way I could know what would happen, right? I can't forgive myself for just giving up on Megan, though. She can't forgive me either, and I don't blame her."

"Damn. I wish things were different."

"Sometimes, I don't think...," Fiona's voice trailed off.

"I need a Root Beer. You want anything?"

Fiona crumpled up the empty cigarette pack in her hand. "Yeah. A pack of Parliaments."

Mike opened the car door and started to get out but Fiona grabbed his arm and stopped him. "You know why I'm in Greenfield, Mike?"

"Not really."

"In 1974, my husband took off to New York with his girlfriend, and I decided to get out of Indiana so I could get a fresh start on life. One day, a few weeks later, my dad took us out on his houseboat and I noticed that his anchor was made by "Greenfield Products" in Greenfield, Ohio. I took that as some kind of sign and decided I needed to move to Greenfield, Ohio and make a better life for me and my kids. So, eight days later, I did just that. I took advice from a fucking boat anchor and look where it's got me."

Mike looked at Fiona and for a moment she thought he was going to cry. Instead, he shook his head slowly and said "Parliaments, right?" Then he finished getting out of his car.

Fiona watched Mike walk into the store. Then she opened the glove box, took Mike's Colt forty-five caliber handgun out from under the pile of napkins, and slipped it into her purse.

PART FIVE

The next day was Saturday. Fiona and two other girls worked giving handjobs to a bunch of guys at an after-hours bachelor party at Maple Creek Country Club. She didn't have any dates on Sunday. Monday morning, she saw a regular client at his house and, that afternoon, another regular and his girlfriend at The Lanes.

On Tuesday, she was scheduled to see a sailor home on leave. She called Jerry and told him she was sick though, so Bonnie Bishop filled in. After calling in sick, Fiona made coffee and started getting things in order.

Fiona woke up Wednesday morning and showered, but skipped the usual hair and makeup routine. She dressed in old jeans and a baggy jacket with the hood pulled up. Checking herself in the mirror, she was startled at how much the reflection did not look like her. *I'm outta here once and for all,* she thought. *No more Jerry Garner, no more Harold Dixon, no more sleazy motel rooms, no more selling myself to men who only want to use me. I'm done. Out of Greenfield forever.* She wasn't sure exactly where she would end up but was sure it wouldn't be worse than where she was.

Before leaving, Fiona took one more look around the apartment. Spotting the photo of Herbie and Megan hanging on the fridge, she took it down and shoved it in her back pocket. Fiona then locked the door behind her and walked out forever.

At eight thirty-six, Fiona pulled into the parking lot at Dixon's Grocery. Only a half dozen cars were scattered around the lot, so she had no problem finding a spot near the front door. Looking through the large plate glass window, she could see a young man organizing empty pop bottles, and a cashier, back towards her register, filing her nails.

A young mother, pushing a cart, came out the door with a little girl riding in front and a boy standing on the end. The girl was laughing and the boy was making race car sounds. It reminded Fiona of shopping trips with Herbie and Megan. How she would give anything to go back.

Fiona shut off the engine and checked her face in the rearview mirror, more out of habit than anything. The face looking back was that of a stranger.

As she walked through the automatic door and into the store, an elderly couple passed her, going in the opposite direction, and smiled. She walked past the young man sorting pop bottles and the cashier filing her nails. Neither seemed to notice.

The woman in the customer service office, who had never spoken to her before, looked up as Fiona walked by and said, "Good morning."

With a smile, Fiona turned towards her and said, "Good morning."

Two teenage girls stood by the time clock, chewing gum and talking, waiting to clock in. Fiona noticed how young they looked. *Babies*, she thought. *I hope they never meet Jerry Garner.*

A voice came over the intercom asking Dick Blevins to come to the meat department. Fiona recognized the voice. It was Harold Dixon. She walked to the meat department, didn't see Harold, and walked on.

As she turned down aisle eleven, Fiona took in the scene before her. Down the left side were toilet bowl cleaners, deodorizers, furniture polish, glass cleaners, and kitchen degreasers. Next to the chemicals were paper towels, and next to them was an assortment of mops, brooms, buckets, brushes, trash cans, and dustpans. Everything you need to keep your home sparkling clean and smelling fresh.

The right side of the aisle was filled with laundry detergent: Tide, Cheer, Wisk, Surf, and Gain. *Why do we need so many options?* Fiona wondered. Next was the Biz, then the bleach, and finally, the fabric softeners. Two pallets of blue plastic jugs of Downey. The stuff whose smell reminded Fiona of her granny's house and soft blankets on a cold night. Glorious Downey. And what do you know? It was on sale. Fiona read the sign to herself. "BUY ONE. GET ONE FREE. WITH A COUPON." *You gotta have a coupon,* Fiona thought. Standing next to the pallet of Downey, straightening jugs and wondering if the sale sign is big enough was none other than the proprietor of Dixon's Grocery. Baby New Year, Class Salutatorian, Master Mason, Ordained Deacon, Man of The Year, renowned Whore Monger, and all-around pillar of the community, Mister Harold Dixon.

Fiona didn't hesitate. She walked towards the Downey display and stopped eight feet short. A tired-looking woman with rollers in her hair walked up beside her and looked at the display. Harold reacted like the barker at a carnival sideshow, holding his bottle of fabric softener and going on about softness, freshness, and coupons. The woman wrinkled her nose, picked up a jug of store-brand fabric softener, and headed for the register.

Harold watched the woman walk away, then turned his attention to Fiona. "Good morning, ma'am. Downy Fabric Softener, buy one, get one free. Coupons are in our weekly flier."

Fiona stared at Harold without responding.

Harold smiled and glanced side to side before looking all around, including behind himself. "Is there something I can help you with, ma'am? Can I help you find something?"

"I'm not here to shop," Fiona replied.

Harold's forehead wrinkled, and he looked confused. "Fiona? Is that you?"

"Why so surprised?"

Harold looked around nervously. "You look... different."

Fiona didn't respond.

"You're not supposed to be here talking to me like this," he whispered. "People can't see us together. I'll pick you up at the motel at three o'clock, and we'll drive to Cincinnati. Now get on out of here."

Fiona smiled.

"Good morning, Mrs. Cochran," Harold said to a tiny old woman pushing her cart down the aisle.

"Can't we talk a minute, Harold?"

"I mean it," Harold whispered. "Get your ass outta

here."

"Or what?"

Harold's face turned red, and beads of sweat appeared on his forehead.

"Today is a special day, Harold."

"You listen to me. I want you out of here right now. You'll regret it if I have to call Jerry."

"Do you know what happened ten years ago today, Harold?"

Harold rolled his eyes. "Is that what this is about? Are you feeling a little depressed today? Do you need some extra attention? I'll give you all the attention you need a little later."

A skinny boy wearing an apron walked up beside Fiona and said, "Excuse me, Mr. Dixon. Rhonda needs you in the deli when you get a minute. I think the freezer is on the blink again."

"I'll be right there," Harold replied, not taking his eyes off Fiona.

The boy walked away.

"You were there when Herbie died," Fiona said calmly.

Harold's face went blank.

"You talked to the police."

"Big deal. I was, uhh… a witness. So what?"

"Cecil Parsons is your nephew."

Harold shifted on his feet, swallowed hard, and looked around

"The cop's wife and son worked for you then, and they work for you now."

A voice on the intercom announced, *"Ladies and gentlemen, please make your way to House Wares, where the Ginsu knife demonstration is set to start in two minutes."*

Harold seethed. "You can't let it go, can you? Ten

years and you can't let it go. Yeah, I was there. I saw the kid standing there with a goofy grin on his face waving at the Ferris Wheel. He didn't bother to look. He just ran into the street and got smashed. It was his fault. End of story. Nobody cares!"

"Well, I care," Fiona hissed; pulling the forty-five out of her purse and leveling it at Harold."

Harold stepped back and nearly tripped over the pallet of Downy. "Now, Fiona. Relax!" He held both arms straight out, palms facing Fiona, in a vain effort to calm her down."

"Well?" Fiona said dryly.

Harold trembled and looked confused. He swallowed hard and tugged at his shirt collar.

"Get on your knees."

"One thousand dollars, Fiona. Just turn and walk away. Go home."

Fiona pulled back the hammer on the gun and felt her finger closing on the trigger. "Stop stalling. On your knees. I want you to know how it feels."

"OK. OK. Just relax," Harold stammered as he got down on his knees, arms still held out like a shield. "Two thousand dollars. Cash."

"You hid everything about Herbie. You've treated me like a misfit toy for years. You've lied, cheated, and stolen your way to the top of this sad, worn-out town. Greenfield reeks with your stench."

"This town wouldn't be anything if not for men like me," Harold said with no hint of humility. "I've always..."

"Shut up."

Harold trembled.

"Pain never goes away, Harold. I mean real pain. Pain in your heart and soul. It never goes away. You can't treat it. All you can do is try to ignore it. Still, no matter how deep you crawl into a bottle or how much you punish yourself. It never lets up. Sunny days and cloudy days are all the same when you're in real pain. They're all dark. You've never felt that kind of pain."

Harold looked up at Fiona and dropped his hands.

"Life's about choices, Harold. Herbie made his, I made mine, and you made yours. All of us could have made different ones, but we didn't. Did we, Harold? The end result? You're looking at it. You're living it."

"Now, you listen to me, Fiona. This has gone far enough. I admit that I've made a few mistakes. Some bad choices if you will. I'm sorry for that. How much do you want? Ten thousand?"

"I don't want any more of your money, Harold. You've given me plenty of that over the years, and it's not done me any good."

"What the Hell do you want then?"

Fiona laughed. "I want you to feel the pain of your choices. Once you feel it, you'll never forget it. Do you know how valuable that is, Harold? You can't put a price tag on something like that."

The intercom rang out, *"Mr. Dixon, please come to the deli."*

Harold looked around. "OK. I feel it. I promise you I feel it, especially in my knees. I'm going to get up now. You go on home, and we'll pretend this never happened."

Harold started to get up.

"You stay right where you're at, you son of a bitch."

Harold looked into the barrel of the forty-five. Sweat rolled down his face and soaked into his starched white collar and blue tie. "I'm tired of playing with you, Fiona. We both know that you don't have the guts to pull that trigger. I'm going to get up, and you're going to walk outta here while you can still walk."

"Don't you move another muscle."

Harold clenched his jaw, and his eyes narrowed. "You fucking whore. You better pull that trigger because if you don't, I will kill you."

"The truth is, Harold, you never did. Not one time."

Harold looked confused. "Never did what?"

"You never made me… you know. Not once."

"That's it, whore!"

KA-BOOM!

The slug drove Harold back into the display of Downey. A stream of blood shot into the air like a geyser from the hole in his forehead. Harold's eyes were open, and his feet convulsed. His mouth moved like it was trying to form words, but none spilled forth. It may have been the first time in his life that Harold Dixon was speechless.

Fiona pointed the pistol at Harold, lying on the floor, and squeezed the trigger over and over until it stopped making noise. One slug hit Harold in the chest, and the others ripped into unsuspecting jugs of Downy Fabric Softener, sending the pink liquid onto the floor, creating a pleasant, homey smell to accompany the grisly scene.

Fiona tucked the pistol back into her purse and walked calmly to the door. The thirty or so people in the store were hurrying here and there. Some ran towards the sounds, not recognizing what it was, and others sought cover, keenly aware of the sound's origin.

No one tried to stop Fiona. Probably because no one believed the quiet-looking woman had anything to do with the disturbance.

As she reached the door, Fiona heard a scream.

"Ahhhhhhh! Mr. Dixon! Someone call the police! I think he's dead!"

Fiona smiled.

When she reached her car. Fiona calmly started it, backed out, and took the rear exit out of the parking lot. She rolled down her window and heard sirens approaching from downtown.

Without really meaning to, Fiona found herself on North Street next to the practice field. She stopped the car where her ten-year-old son had lost his life. She wondered why there wasn't an X on the road, marking the spot like there was in Dallas where JFK was shot. *Was John Kennedy's life worth remembering more than Herbie Farmer's?*

Fiona turned the car into the alley towards her old house on Lafayette Street. She looked at the backyard, and for a moment, she saw Herbie and Megan playing. They looked happy. She heard their laughs and saw their smiles. The sun was warm on her face.

The driveway next to her old house was empty, so she parked and got out of the car. She pressed her hands and face to the kitchen window and looked at the same cabinet over the stove where she had kept her tip jar. She could still picture the worn five-dollar bill she gave Herbie that day. It didn't occur until then that she never got that five-dollar bill back with Herbie's personal effects. She got his pocketknife, a pack of Teaberry chewing gum, a plastic ring, and six dollars and thirty-three cents in cash. That worn five-dollar bill wasn't included, though. How strange.

A yellow cat rubbed against Fiona's leg, then lay on the driveway and scratched his back on the gray asphalt. She smiled and said, "John Boy? Is it really you?" When she reached down to pet him, the cat ran away.

Sirens were still whaling as Fiona got back into her car and drove off.

The car seemed to be on autopilot as Fiona's mind went blank. It drove itself for two miles across town before Fiona became aware. She found herself parked in the middle of an intersection. The car was running, and the radio was on. *"You're listening to WSRW Radio. Coming to you from the city of the hills, Hillsboro, Ohio. We just got a call from our good friend, Clint Walker, at Greenfield Grain and Hay. He told us there has been a mass shooting at Dixon's Grocery in Greenfield this morning. Clint didn't have many details but said there are at least five dead and many more wounded. We will bring you more details as they become available. Until then, here's Conway Twitty singing "Slow Hand."*

PART SIX

Fiona looked around and realized she was parked in the street at the intersection of South Second and Summerfield. She got out of the car, engine running.

Before she walked away, Fiona retrieved an envelope from her purse. It was addressed to:

Megan Farmer
941 Finley Street
Tipton, IN 46072

She held the envelope to her lips for several seconds, then dropped it in the mailbox on the corner and walked on.

A group of young boys sitting on a front porch drinking Kool-Aid and telling lies watched her walk by.

Three men standing across the street in front of King's Barber Shop saw her and wondered who she was. One commented that he had seen her before but couldn't remember where.

A truck nearly hit her as she walked past the feed mill,

and the driver honked his horn. Fiona didn't seem to notice.

When she got to the railroad tracks, Fiona suddenly felt free. It was a feeling that she hadn't felt in ten years, and it was good. The guilt, the memories, the mistakes, and the poor decisions all seemed to fade away. A voice from inside told Fiona to pick left or right. *Either way is fine,* the voice said. *Both will take you there.* Fiona chose left.

The smell of creosote was unmistakable to anyone who had ever walked along a railroad track on a hot summer day. Fiona adjusted her stride so she could step on the ties and remembered her childhood in Indiana, and how she would walk the railroad tracks from her house outside of town into Tipton. It was probably no more than a quarter mile, but it felt like several miles to her then. As she passed the hog pens at the slaughterhouse, she stepped onto the rail and balanced herself like she had seen the trapeze artists do at the circus when it came to town.

When she came to the trestle, Fiona paused and could hear the rapids of Paint Creek running below. She started to cross, using the walking platform, and heard the faint whistle of an approaching train. She turned to look behind her and saw the small bright headlamp leading the train towards her. She wished she had a penny to lay on the tracks.

Fiona stood still as the train approached. The heat rising from the tracks made the engine look surreal. She felt the vibration and heard the train's whistle call out. She closed her eyes. The smell of cotton candy and the sound of a calliope filled her head.

Fiona thought of Herbie and Megan and how much she loved them. For a brief but distinct moment, she was overcome with sorrow. When she opened her eyes, she saw Herbie on the other side of the tracks, standing on the edge of the trestle, and she felt good again. He seemed to hover like his feet weren't touching the ground. He was smiling and beckoned her to come. *Here I am, mom!*

The train blasted its horn.

A smile crossed Fiona's face, and her heart filled with joy. "Mommy's coming, baby! Mommy's coming!"

MEDIOCRE MOON

Just past midnight on June 30, 1993, I left the right side of the roadway in a seventy-one Plymouth Roadrunner, traveling nearly one hundred miles per hour, and spent the night in a southern Ohio cow pasture.

The car had drifted left of center, and as I tried to bring it back into the right lane, I overcompensated, and it shot over the ditch and through the wire fence. The car tore through the muddy field, went airborne for fifty-three feet, landed, and began to flip end over end. I wasn't wearing a seat belt, so I bounced around the front of the car a bit before being squeezed through the space between the roof and the top of the bench seat. I was six-foot-three and went about two hundred sixty-five pounds at the time, so it was a tight fit, to say the least. After chewing me up, the car shit me out the passenger side window. I went airborne for seventy-seven feet, hit the ground, and rolled twenty-nine more feet before I slammed into a large bale of hay, ricocheted off, and landed flat on my back.

Route 28, east of Greenfield, is straight as an arrow

and rises slightly for about a mile before it flattens out all the way to Lyndon. There are clusters of houses lining the road now, but it was mostly corn and soybeans with occasional pastures full of goats or cattle back in the early nineties.

When I was a kid, my family made monthly Saturday trips west on 28 to Chillicothe so we could go to this little place on Bridge Street for milkshakes and greasy burgers and so my mom could shop at Rink's Bargain City. Later, I learned to drive on 28 and all the little roads that ran off it.

I was as drunk as a happy hour priest when I wrecked, but that wasn't what caused it. You see, Stevie Ray Vaughn was on the radio singing "Pride and Joy," and I went to turn up the volume when he got to the part about the guy getting mean because someone messes with his girl. That's my favorite part of the song, and I always turn it up and sing out loud. Well, when I reached for the volume button, the cherry from my cigarette fell off and onto my seat. I swatted at it, trying to keep it from burning a hole in the vinyl, and when I did, I jerked the wheel. The rest is history.

As the car shot off the road, I realized what was happening and sobered up quickly. My senses were suddenly operating at what you might call peak performance. Stevie Ray was still singing and playing as the car bottomed out, and I slammed my head into the roof. When I started flipping end over end, I thought to myself, *this is gonna hurt like hell.*

I'll never forget the sound the car made as it was torn apart. It reminded me of the screech that Godzilla made as he ripped the shit out of Tokyo in those old Japanese movies. It was loud and horrible but muffled like it was underwater and playing at three-quarters speed. I rolled around the car in slow motion, crashing into the steering wheel and getting sprayed in the face with chunks of broken glass. I went shoulder-first into the passenger side front pillar, then shot back across the car ass-first into the driver's side door. As crazy as it sounds, there was hardly any pain. Isn't that some shit? I felt the impacts, but they were muted and dull. Continuing to flip, I remember looking down at the gear shift and thinking, *if I can hold onto that shifter, I'll ride this out and not get beat to death.* All this chaos was going on around me, glass flying everywhere, chunks of dirt and grass plastering my face, things shifting around in my body, bones cracking, and I was concentrating as hard as I could on that pistol grip shifter.

At one point, the chaos seemed to stop. Godzilla wasn't roaring, and the jolts and impacts subsided. I had the sensation of flying as the night air blew past my face. It was peaceful and almost serene. The moon appeared through the window. It was bright and somewhere between half-full and full. I'd say it was an eighty percent moon. Not anything spectacular. Nothing that anyone would take a picture of, for sure. *A second-rate mediocre moon, perfect for the situation,* I thought, as the bell sounded for round two.

I don't recall being squeezed into the back seat. I just kind of appeared back there. Like I said, I was a big guy then. Me and some buddies had been making regular weekend trips to Tijuana to buy steroids from this sketchy clinic two blocks from the border. They had stanozolol, boldenone, nandrolone, and other shit I had never heard of. For two hundred dollars, we'd get a shot in the ass, then we'd go sit in this little place down the street called "Cantina Miguel's" and have a couple beers. We'd wait until this little boy, who must have been about nine or ten, showed up with a brown paper bag containing a dozen vials with handwritten labels that said, "El Toro." I heard it was animal-grade testosterone that they used to shoot up fighting bulls, but I don't know if that's true or not. We'd smuggle it back into California in bags of coffee or rolled up in tacos. I put on thirty two pounds of pure muscle in less than four months. My balls shriveled up like raisins, but I could squat a tank and looked like a million bucks. No matter, somehow, I still ended up in that back seat.

As I was lying on the floorboard in the back, I swear I saw an empty Little Kings bottle hovering above me. I shit you not; it was suspended in midair like something out of a magic show. I wondered if maybe I had died and hadn't realized it yet. Maybe my Hell was to get the shit beat out of me for eternity in the back seat of this damn car, and maybe that Little Kings bottle was there to taunt me.

I don't know how long I lay in that field before realizing I was there. I must have gotten KO'd while watching the hovering bottle. I could have been out ten seconds or ten days. I had no way of knowing. When I became aware, I was gagging and coughing because my mouth was full of dirt and grass. I started talking out loud, and I remember thinking, *whose voice is that? It sounds like he's choking on a shit sandwich.*

"What time is it?"
"Where's my car?"
"I'm gonna miss formation."
"Gunny's gonna be up my ass."
"Has anyone seen Smitty?"
"Maria! Where's Maria?"

At first, I couldn't figure out how I got where I was, and I tried to stand up. My body wasn't having it, though.

Nothing but my head and right arm would move.

I fell asleep, and when I woke up, my head hurt so bad I threw up. I felt it coming, so I turned to the right and sent a stream of beer, bourbon, and bile shooting into the night air. My throat burned like Hell, but it felt good to let it go.

"I wrecked my fuckin' car. You've got to be shittin' me."

Gradually things started to make some sense. I remembered having supper with my brother Will, then going back to my parent's house to shower and change clothes. Around seven-fifteen, I drove out to the Mini Bar and ran into my high school science teacher, Mr. Dunkle. We shot pool and drank a couple beers, then got a table by the jukebox and had another beer and a shot of Maker's. We talked about how he hated teaching science almost as much as I hated taking it and compared our lists of the hottest girls in my senior class. I liked the dark-haired girls with big tits, and, it turns out, old Dunk preferred the skinny blondes. As we talked, I couldn't take my eyes off the giant ass booger in his nose, moving in and out with every breath he took. It was gross, but he was buying, so I just tried to ignore it and enjoy my drinks.

I left the bar around nine o'clock and drove back into town. My old buddy, Mikey Allen, was coming out of Furio's Pizza, so I laid on the horn and pulled over. Mikey got a pint of Wild Turkey, two cans of Coke, a bag of weed, and a thirty - eight caliber revolver out of his truck and jumped in with me. We drove the back roads between Greenfield and Leesburg while we killed the Turkey, smoked a joint, and shot up some signs. Then I dropped Mikey off at his truck. That must have been about eleven - fifty or so.

I was pretty wasted by then and almost went back to

my parent's house to crash. Instead, I decided to drive out 28 to Lyndon and see what the car could do. I had just bought it a few days before, in Hillsboro, and had yet to open it up. That turned out to be a bad decision.

I pulled onto Jefferson Street, did a U-turn in front of the police station, ran the red light at Washington Street, and headed out of town. As I got to the bridge over Paint Creek, I lit a cigarette, cracked the window, and punched the pedal to the floor into Ross County. The radio was on Q-FM 96, and they were just finishing up a set of three from AC/DC as I passed Thrifton Road. I was doing almost ninety at that point and eased off the gas as I went through the flashing light at the intersection of Route 41. Clearing the intersection, I punched it again and watched the speedometer hit a hundred. I drove about a quarter mile when I saw headlights coming toward me and backed it off a little. Stevie Ray Vaughn was just coming on the radio.

Laying there in the field, I heard a train whistle in the distance, and I thought of the sleepouts me, Mikey Allen, and Joe Miller had in the backyard when we were kids. We slept in this musty old canvas tent, and the sound of approaching trains on the B&O always made me feel like I was in the presence of ghosts. It was like the darkness, and the lonely train whistles caused them to rise up and move amongst those who took the time to notice them. I felt them in the field that night, and it gave me some sort of weird comfort that old friends had come to sit with me and perhaps take me with them when they left.

"Holy shit, what the fuck is that?"

I heard heavy breathing, followed by grunts and snorts, and it made me think of the scene in "Ghost" where Carl gets impaled by the glass from the broken window and dies. His spirit rises from his body, and he doesn't know what's happening until the demons appear out of the shadows and drag him, kicking and screaming, to Hell. Had the demons come for me?

Something was standing two feet from me, and it let out a long deep moan that sounded like a foghorn, followed by a snotty exhale. From the light of the mediocre moon, I could see a large white cow swinging her head, snorting, and stomping the ground with her front feet. I began to worry that I'd be trampled, and I started to wave my right arm around in the air as I turned my head from side to side, trying to scare the cow away. That didn't seem to faze her, so I tried yelling at her, but the dirt in my mouth made it hard to do. Plus, anything beyond a whisper hurt my chest. "Get away! Don't step on me!" I pleaded. She sniffed the air, took a gigantic shit, and stared at me. I heard more cows moving around me. They walked near but didn't pay much attention to me. They seemed more interested in eating grass, shitting, and pissing. I was literally in a world of shit.

I tried again to move my legs, but they wouldn't cooperate, and neither would my left arm. My right arm moved, though, and I became almost fascinated by that. For some reason, I kept putting my hand in front of my face, so I could count my fingers. I'm not sure why I did that, but it occurred to me that I should use those fingers to clean some of the dirt out of my mouth. It was then that I noticed what looked kinda like a person's leg lying next to me, but I couldn't quite make it out. So I didn't worry about it.

I wondered what Maria was doing at that moment back in California. Could she see that shitty mediocre moon shining down on me and the cows? Maybe she was thinking of me and wondering what I was doing. *Maybe she misses me,* I thought as I drifted off to sleep.

I shook myself awake, calling out for my mom. I had dreamt that I had fallen off my bicycle and scraped my hands and knees. They were bleeding, and I thought I was going to die. I was little. Six years old, maybe seven. I was crying, and I wanted my mom. She came to me, but she was old. Much older than she should have been. I felt terrible that I was bleeding, and I told her I was sorry. I asked her to sit down and rest, and I brought her a glass of iced tea. My hands and knees were still bleeding, and I wanted my mom to help me, but she couldn't because she was old and needed my help. Suddenly I was grown up. I handed my mom the glass of iced tea, but I noticed it had turned to blood. I cried out, "Mom, help me!".

You read about men calling for their mothers as they bleed out on the battlefield, rot from the inside out in a hospital bed far from home, or lie dying in a field, drunk and covered in cow shit. It occurred to me then that sons don't belong to their mothers. Mothers belong to their sons. We are formed in our mother's womb, and we share our first heartbeat with her. When we are born, our mothers hold us to their breast. A son should be so blessed as to die before his mother if only so she can hold him to her breast and share his last heartbeat as well.

Sprawled out in that field, I saw my mother, standing with my brother Jack, looking at me from behind a tree. I called out to them, but they didn't answer. Maybe they weren't there. I'm not sure.

I wasn't a Christian then, but I felt the need to cry out to God. I didn't know how to go about it, so I thought of my granny. Outside of her and my grandpa, my family wasn't what you would call Godly people. Granny sometimes took me to Sunday School and always signed me up for Vacation Bible School in the summer. She wrote poems about Jesus and would read them to us grandkids. I remember one called "The Master Is Coming." It was about being prepared to meet Jesus and having a strong enough relationship with him that you'd be able to recognize him when he showed up. I cried out into the dark, "Jesus, help me!" I knew that Jesus was God's son, but I had heard someone say once that Jesus <u>was</u> God. That made no sense to me at the time because I hadn't been washed in the blood yet, so I asked them both for help.

"God, I need you! Are you listening?"

I thought about how bad of a kid I had been and all the trouble I had gotten into. My parents were forty years old when I was born. That's too old to have your fourth kid, and I made them pay a heavy price for their lackadaisical attitude towards birth control. Me and Mikey used to fuck things up with impunity. We egged the neighbor's cars, shoplifted from Willie Bobb's store, and painted cuss words on the sidewalk. One Sunday morning, we threw rocks through every window in the feed mill next to our house just for kicks. The old man was constantly paying for the stuff we destroyed to keep the cops from getting involved.

One time, Jack found this little yellow kitten and named it Sundown. He really liked that cat, and he took good care of it. I got annoyed one day because it kept following me around the yard. So I beat it to death with a tomato stake and hid it under a bush. Another time, I threw a stray cat into a burning trash can. Mom had to call the dog catcher to come and shoot it.

I remembered Mom pacing the floor, crying, and asking God why he was punishing her. She suffered more than anyone because of me. She was always on duty and rarely got a break. Dad worked in Columbus, and when he got home, he ate supper, watched the news, then slept on the couch until bedtime. On weekends, he ran around wheeling and dealing, playing cards, and generally ignoring the rest of the family, except for those weekend trips to Chillicothe. Mom, though, cooked and cleaned and took care of me and my brothers. I got most of her attention because I was the youngest, and it wasn't always the good kind. Mom didn't mess around and didn't hesitate to use the razor strop hanging in the dining room closet to get her point across. I wondered if sometimes she regretted my being born. I wondered if she loved me. I wondered if she hated me. She's my mom, so I figured she'd break down at my funeral. She'd sob, and the old man wouldn't know how to comfort her. I wondered, though, if at night, when it got dark and quiet and sleep wouldn't come if she'd feel some relief that I was gone. Would she dream about me?

I told myself I would be a better kid if I had another chance. *But I'm not a kid anymore. I'm a man now,* I thought. *I do rotten man things, like drink and smoke, fight in bars, smuggle contraband into the country, slip out of restaurants without paying the bill, look at porn, and fuck whores. I lie and cheat. I carry guns and drive fast cars. Being a better kid wasn't an option now.* I began to cry. Then I fell asleep again and dreamed of Maria.

You know how sometimes when you first wake up, there's that split second that you think everything is good? You forget that your best friend died the day before, that it's Monday, not Saturday, or that your girlfriend caught you fucking her sister. For just a second, you forget. Then you remember, and your heart sinks. That kept happening to me. I kept falling asleep, and I would wake up and think I was in the sack with Maria, on the couch at Shorty's place, or in my rack back at Camp Pendleton, but only for a second. Just long enough to think, *damn, what a dream.* Then I'd realize I was lying in a field dying. Talk about a kick to the jewels.

"*Why am I crying?*"

I got to thinking about how strange it was that I wasn't in a lot of pain. My head hurt some, though, and when I tried to run my fingers through my hair, I noticed it was gooey from what I assumed was blood. Something hard and sharp stuck out of my face between my left eye and ear. At first, I thought it was bone, but I figured out it was a chunk of glass.

The mosquitos and flies were terrible, and they swarmed my face. I slapped at them with my one working hand, but they just kept coming. It reminded me of the sand fleas at Parris Island and how our Drill Instructors wouldn't let us kill the bastards. Those motherfuckers wouldn't even let us wear bug spray. We just suffered. It was part of our training. It "built character" and "instilled discipline," they said. That training was coming in handy now, and I was thankful for it.

Random things started running through my head. Some of it was funny bullshit that made me laugh out loud.

Did my Drill Instructors make all that crap up, or were they working from a script?

When Big Dick Richards was a baby, did his mother call him Baby Dick Richards?

As a boy, I liked Ginger. As a man, I LOVE Mary Ann.

Did aliens really invade the moon in 1969?

I remembered the time when I was about eleven or twelve years old, and me and Mikey cornered Jack's best friend, Donnie Kessler, on our front porch and horsewhipped the shit out of him with six-foot maple switches while Jack laughed and egged us on. Donnie was dancing and hollering like his ass was on fire. He wore the welts from that beating for a week.

Other thoughts weren't so funny, and they gave me cause for great concern.

How much have I bled, and how much blood do I have left to bleed?

I'll be just another piece of roadkill to the buzzards and crows. No different than a raccoon or a stray dog.

The pussy that I've had pales in comparison to the pussy that I'll never get.

My dress blues are still at the cleaners in Oceanside. How long before they get pawned?

I thought of the time I made a Valentine's card for Karen Biscotti. She was the prettiest girl in seventh grade, and I was really starting to become aware of girls. One night before Valentine's Day, I used construction paper, ribbon, lace, and colored markers to make the best Valentine's card ever constructed by a boy my age. The next day, I put on a dress shirt and drenched myself in Brut before going to school. I saw Karen in the hallway between first and second period, so I handed her the card and even managed to say, "Hi, Karen." I felt like I was on top of the world, and I was sure she would fall in love with me, and we'd probably eat lunch together and hold hands in the courtyard every day after school. Instead, she waited until we were walking into the cafeteria and made a big production of ripping up the card and throwing it in the trash while her bitch friends laughed and made fun of me. I was embarrassed, and I felt small. That night I thought about killing myself but decided against it.

Four years later, to the day, Karen hanged herself in her bedroom closet after Pete Simmons dumped her for Jennifer Portman. I remember feeling some form of redemption when I heard the news. *She got what she deserved,* I thought. It wasn't until I saw her parents accept her diploma at graduation that I realized how embarrassed and small Karen must have felt that day in her closet. I'll never forget her mother's sobs and the look of defeat on her father's face. I was overcome with grief, and when I got home, I went to my room, laid down on my bed, and cried. Then, I went out and got drunk.

I felt myself falling asleep again, and I wondered if I'd wake up this time. The cows were grunting and moaning as I drifted away, and I felt a cool breeze blowing across my face. A dog barked in the distance, and occasional cars buzzed by on 28. It was peaceful, and I thought it wouldn't be so bad if I stayed here forever.

My eyes opened, and I realized that the sun was starting to rise on my left. For the first time, I got a clear view of my surroundings. I was in a grassy field, flat to my left and right, with a small hill rising in the direction my foot was pointing. There was a big half-eaten bale of hay about ten feet from me on my right and a large trough with a spigot and a coil of green hose lying next to it. A few shabby trees were scattered here and there, including one that had a dozen or so of those foil happy birthday balloons stuck in its branches. Off to my left was a small barn and an old silo crumbling into the ground. A rusted-out pickup truck was sitting half-hidden by the silo with dry weeds growing up around it. How long had I been stretched out amongst the cows? If Stevie Ray Vaughn serenaded me off the road just past midnight, I guessed I'd been lying there for about six hours or so.

Through the soft light, I could see the cows lying around me like they were on guard duty. I counted nine, but I figured there were more. It made me think of baby Jesus lying in the manger, and I wondered if God allowed the cows to shit in his presence or if he suspended that so as not to be a distraction.

While looking at that rusted-out pickup, I determined that there was definitely a leg lying next to me, and it worried me a little. I kept trying to remember who was with me. Smitty? Shorty? Maybe one of the baldheads just in from Comm School? I couldn't remember. Whoever it was, he was wearing a pair of soft Tony Lamas, just like mine. For a second, I thought it must have been that cabron, Perez. Then I remembered that he only wore cheap ass Dingos. The leg was lying so the outer ankle was pointing to the sky, and the heel of those Tony Lamas was facing me. It was wearing tight faded blue jeans, in the Dwight Yoakam style, just like I was wearing.

I followed the seam of the jeans, from the heel of the boot, up the calf, all the way to the knee, where the leg took a strange turn, like it had an extra joint in it or something, and finally to my own left hip. "Holy shit! My leg!" I panicked for the first time since the cherry blew off my Winston. That was MY leg, twisted at a bizarre angle and lying at my side. No wonder I couldn't move it. Any attachment that leg had to any other part of my body was superficial at best.

That realization, and the dark turning to light, seemed to put my situation into urgent terms. I was lying in a field next to what used to be my leg, unable to move my left arm or anything below the waist, my face and head swollen like a pumpkin, my insides throbbing and aching, and most of my blood soaked into the cow shit laden ground beneath me. I was a young man and had a lot of life to live. I needed to get the Hell outta there.

The sun was up now, and I figured it must be about seven o'clock. I couldn't move, I couldn't yell, and I had no way of signaling anyone. I'd have to hope that someone saw me. Maybe the farmer who owned these cows would come out to do whatever cow farmers do with cows and haul me outta there on a tractor. Perhaps someone would see the hole in the fence and my car sitting in the field and call 911. A crop duster might fly over and see me sprawled out on the ground and radio for help. Or maybe my guardian angel, if I had one, would pop out of the clouds and whisk me off to the happy place.

It was too early for anyone to miss me yet. Mom and Dad would be up soon, though. They would notice my car wasn't parked next to the house but wouldn't think much of it. It might be Noon before Mom called my brothers to ask if they had seen me. She'd get worried when I didn't show up at five o'clock for supper. Around six o'clock, she'd call everyone again, and by nine-thirty or so, she'd ask my brothers to go driving around town to see if they could find me. By tomorrow morning, she'd call the cops to report me missing. By then, I'd be cold and stiff, and the buzzards would be circling in anticipation of a good meal. I kept thinking about...

"What was that?"

I could have sworn I heard a voice. Maybe it was a cow or the wi...

"Listen!"

There was no doubt in my mind. I heard a voice. It was faint and distant, but I heard a voice. "Help me," I muttered.

The voice was clear now. "Are you okay?" It was a woman's voice.

The woman suddenly appeared over me. She dropped down on her knees and looked me over. "I'm going to help you," she said. "Try not to move."

I'll never forget her bright blue eyes and how good she smelled. It took a moment, but I realized that I knew her. Her name was Amber Ashby. She was three years ahead of me in school, and she smiled at me one time when we walked past each other on the steps between classes. She wouldn't remember me or that encounter, but I never forgot it.

"Where are you hurt?" she asked.

"Everywhere," I replied.

She was dressed in a white uniform and a blue sweater. She was wearing small diamond earrings, and she had a wedding ring on her finger. The name tag on her blouse said, "Amber White - R.T. - Chillicothe Regional Medical Center."

"How long have you been out here?" she asked.

"What time is it?" I answered.

She looked at her watch and said, "Seven thirty-one."

"Well, about seven and a half hours. Am I going to die?"

She looked at my twisted leg and said, "I'm going for help. I want you to lie still. Try not to move, okay?"

She took off her sweater, laid it on my chest, and tucked it under my chin. She might have touched my cheek with her hand. Or maybe she didn't.

"I won't be gone long," she said. "I promise."

I felt myself slipping off to sleep again. The scent of Amber's perfume filled my head, and I started to dream of Maria.

"I'm here," the voice said.

I opened my eyes and whispered, "Maria?"

Amber was kneeling beside me again, and I heard sirens far off in the distance. She had brought a blanket and covered me with it. It was blue and smelled like the large cedar chest in my mom's bedroom, where she kept the extra sheets and blankets. She took hold of my wrist and looked at her watch, and I wondered if my pulse increased a little. She continued to hold my hand, and I asked her again if I was going to die. Her eyes were wet, and she said, "It's going to be okay. They're almost here." The sirens grew louder, then cut off, and I heard doors slamming, people talking, and more sirens approaching.

I recognized the next face hovering over me as Doug Harper, a Greenfield cop who had told me to get out of places I didn't belong and go home at least a hundred times when I was a kid. "Matt Connor? Is that you?" he asked as he knelt in the cow shit to have a look.

"I wish it wasn't," I replied.

I heard an engine rumbling behind me and voices advising, "Watch that hole! Don't get it stuck! Not so fast."

Doors opened and shut, and Amber's face was replaced by that of a middle-aged woman named Doris. Doris looked like Greg "The Hammer" Valentine, and I imagined her dropping an elbow on my face and rolling me up for the pin. Instead, she removed the blanket, took my blood pressure, and listened to my chest with a stethoscope.

A guy, not much older than me, knelt by my head and shined a light into my eyes. "Can you tell me your name?" he asked.

"Uhh, Matt Connor. What's yours?"

"Wayne," he replied as he put me in a neck brace.

"How old are you, Matt?"

The question caught me off guard, and at first, I couldn't remember how old I was. A few seconds went by, and I answered, "I think I'm twenty. No, wait, I'm twenty-one. I turned twenty-one in December."

Doris wiped mud out of my mouth and nose and started cutting off my clothes with a pair of scissors. She stripped me naked except for the pant leg and boot on what used to be my left leg. I felt a little self-conscious laying there, and I hoped I'd at least chub up a little for the ladies. Wayne must have sensed my concern, and he covered my crotch with Amber's sweater.

Other people were moving about, talking on the radio, and looking me over. I asked Wayne what was going on, and he said, "We're calling in a helicopter to get you out of here."

"Wayne, am I going to die?" I asked him.

"The helicopter is on its way," he said, not looking at me.

After what seemed like forever, I heard a pop, and white smoke blew across the field. I guessed they were marking a landing spot for the helicopter, and I could hear it approaching within a few seconds.

Wayne told me to close my eyes, and he shielded my face with an orange poncho as the helicopter landed and sent grass, dirt, and cow shit flying through the air. I saw stampeding cattle as the rotors slowed and then stopped.

A guy in a flight suit, carrying a bag, plopped down beside me, talked to Doris and Wayne for a moment, then put a stethoscope on my chest. He moved it around a few times, nodded, and wrote something down in a notebook. He was the flight paramedic, and his name was Rob.

A tall red-haired woman, also in a flight suit, was busy attaching wires to my chest. She had a stern, business-like appearance, but she smiled when she noticed me looking at her. After conferring with Rob, she jabbed an IV into my arm and started emptying syringes into the line. When she finished, she held my hand. I learned later that her name was Jill. She was the flight nurse, and she died in a hit-and-run accident while crossing a busy street in downtown Columbus, just two days after helping me in that field. She was thirty years old. I've always hoped someone was there to hold her hand.

Things started to get a little fuzzy as the painkillers running through my veins took effect. I remember Rob telling me that I might experience a little discomfort while they stabilized my left leg. I told him, "Hell, Doc, you could saw me in half, and I wouldn't feel a damn thing."

As they put an air cast on my leg, I saw Amber standing near the bale of hay. Her blonde hair was pulled up on top of her head, and she reminded me of a picture of Jayne Mansfield that I had seen once on one of those bullshit newspapers in the checkout lane at Kmart. I started to imagine how she looked naked but shook the thought out of my head because she saved my life, and it felt disrespectful. We made eye contact, and she smiled and gave me a thumbs-up. I tried to smile back, but I'm not sure I did.

They put me on a stretcher, and I felt like I was going to vomit. When they started me towards the helicopter, I looked to my right and saw my car for the first time. It lay on its top a good distance back towards the road, roof crushed, tires busted, and covered in mud. Various parts were scattered here and there. Behind it, on Route 28, I could see cars stopped in both directions. People were standing on the shoulder watching, and I wished I could wave and thank them for coming out.

As I was being loaded into the helicopter, Harper, the cop, said, "Good luck, Matt. I'll go see your parents, and I'll be praying for you." Rob and Jill climbed in with me. Rob closed the door and gave a nod to the pilot. The blades started turning, and in a few seconds, we were airborne and headed to Columbus.

It was bright inside the helicopter. I had an oxygen mask on my face, and tubes and wires ran everywhere.

The monitors were chirping and flashing, and I could hear the blades cutting the air.

I was exhausted and started to doze off, but before I did, I asked no one in particular, "Am I going to die?"

Jill pushed another syringe into my IV and said, "You're in good hands."

A warm feeling rushed over me, and I smiled. Within seconds I dozed off and dreamt of Maria.

MEALS ON WINGS

I've been livin' in a two-room apartment over top of the Temple of The Lord Church on Tenth Street for the past five months. The church took me in after my latest stint in the Highland County Jail as part of a state-funded holy program to help petty criminals see the light. In exchange for free room and board, plus a two hundred dollar a month allowance, I made a vow to stay straight and take on Jesus as my savior. Plus, I have to do odd jobs around the church like cleanin', paintin', and mowin'. The *Daily Times* did a story about it and put a picture of me, with Brother Lloyd and Sister Irene, on the front page. The headline said, "Local Church Helps Ex Con Turn From Sin." I cut it out and taped it to my bathroom door.

I go to church twice on Sundays and once on Wednesdays.

One Sunday mornin' each month, I stand by the door smilin', shakin' everyone's hand as they come in, and tellin' folks how good it is to see 'em. I even tell a few that I love 'em.

Every Friday at six a.m. I go with Brother Lloyd to the

men's bible study at the Red Rooster Cafe, where we drink coffee and talk about Democrats, THE Ohio State Buckeyes, and Greenfield's pothole problem.

I'm supposed to read the Bible every evenin' for at least an hour. And I try to do it. I swear I do. They had me start with the "Gospel of John" and the "Book of Acts." Now, I'm in "Romans" and "Genesis." Next will be "Psalms" and "Proverbs." Sometimes my mind wanders. When that happens, I turn to "Revelation" and read about dragons, beasts, and angels blowin' trumpets. Doin' so tends to get me back on track. I memorize a verse or two every week, but I don't usually know what they mean. That seems good enough though, because when I stand up on Sunday mornin' and say 'em, everyone smiles, hollers "Amen," and says "That's right," while noddin' their head up and down.

When I'm finished, Brother Lloyd cries, prays for the sinners, and talks about harvestin' the low-hanging fruit. I always know he is talkin' about me, and it makes me feel kinda good to hear him say it.

Three months ago, they started givin' me the keys to the church van every Wednesday evenin', even though I don't have a driver's license, so I can deliver meals to the elderly shut-ins and others who are too sick, too crippled or too lazy to come to church. They call it "Meals on Wings." I like doin' it because it gets me out of the Wednesday service and allows me the opportunity to see people outside the congregation, who, let's face it, can be a little crazy-eyed sometimes, if you know what I mean.

There are two stops on my route that I especially look forward to. The first is Mr. Hannigan on Mirabeau Street. He died a month after I started deliverin', but his name has never been taken off the meal list. His niece, Cheyenne, who had cared for him, still lives there, so I take her the food. After she eats, we listen to music, smoke a bowl, and drink a beer. It's almost like a date, 'cept I never kiss her or anything like that. I want to, but she seems content with the free meal and the buzz, so I leave it at that.

My other favorite stop is Mrs. Dunham on Pine Street. She was seventy-nine years old when I met her. She's eighty now. Six months ago, she twisted her back and wrenched her knee when she fell off her back porch. Her granddaughter had the foresight to schedule monthly appointments for Mrs. Dunham at The Greenfield Pain Clinic, where Dr. Mehmet Kaplan prescribes liberal doses of OxyContin to control her pain.

Mrs. Dunham likes me to read the Bible to her when I come. It don't matter what I read. She says, "They are all God's words. None are any less important than the others."

So, I read my favorite verses from "Leviticus", "Jonah", and "Revelation."

She puts her hands up in the air and says "Hallelujah" and "Thank you, Jesus" while I read. Then she says a prayer and gives me a handful of Oxys for my shoulder and back pain, which I mention to her occasionally. Sometimes, she gives me a whole bottle if I ask. Other times, when I don't want to trouble her, I just help myself. Mrs. Dunham is a lovely lady.

There are twelve more stops on my weekly route. I don't look forward to those nearly as much, though. Most of those folks just look at me through the window and tell me to leave the food on the porch and go away. A few will invite me in and ask me about people I've never heard of and whether this person or that person still goes to church. One man asked me if the church had a new phone number because nobody answers when he calls.

These folks seem lonely, and I try to cheer them up a little. I think my missing teeth and knuckle tattoos make them a little nervous, though, and I can understand that. I always mention these folks to Brother Lloyd. He says he'll try to get one of the Deacons to stop by soon, if they have time.

The last time I was at Mrs. Dunham's house, her granddaughter, a fat girl with long yellow hair and black roots, was there. Her name is Heather. After I did my Bible readin', Heather asked me to step outside, where we talked about her grandmother's pain meds. We discussed tryin' to use the bounty of OxyContin sat before us to do some good work for the community. We decided that from now on, Mrs. Dunham's house would be my second stop. (My first stop would be Mr. Hannigan's, of course). I'd tend to Mrs. Dunham like I always do, then Heather would go with me and help with my deliveries.

With Heather's help, I diversified and grew the route a little. It immediately went from fourteen to eighteen stops, then to twenty-five, finally to forty-two and sometimes forty-six. The new stops don't get food; they just leave a donation that Heather picks up from under a rock, inside a flowerpot, or between seat cushions on the porch swing. In exchange, Heather leaves a sandwich bag that holds their blessing.

Heather gives me thirty percent of the total donations. I anonymously give ten percent of my thirty percent to the church. Brother Lloyd is pleased about the uptick in tithes and offerings. In fact, he's usin' it as an example of God's love in a new series of sermons on reapin' the rewards of your good works.

Honestly, my life is pretty good right now. I'm a creature of change though, and I'm not sure how long I'll stay around. Brother Lloyd wants me to start spendin'

Saturday evenings standin' outside The Village Pump holdin' a sign warnin' folks that Jesus is comin' soon. With winter just around the corner, I'll have to think about it.

MORRIS DELANEY AIN'T NO SISSY
PART 1

My name is Morris Delaney. Morris Len Delaney. I know that sounds like a sissy name, especially nowadays, but I ain't no sissy. There weren't any sissies on the south end of Greenfield, Ohio, in the 1960s, and I'd be willing to bet there ain't too many today.

I reckon October 8, 1998, was the saddest day of my life. When I got home from work that day, I had a message on the answering machine from my sister, Maureen, letting me know our mom had died. She had worked in her garden for a couple hours that morning, came inside for lunch, laid down for a nap, and never woke up.

I'd been working six days a week at Muddy's Tire and Oil, busting lug nuts and changing filters, so I wasn't looking forward to an unplanned cross-country drive. But I took a quick shower, packed a bag, called my boss to ask for a few days off, and jumped in the Cadillac. It was one thousand two hundred and sixty-three miles from my home in Cheyenne, Wyoming, to Greenfield, and I figured the sooner I left, the sooner I'd get there.

Around midnight, I found myself bellied up to the counter at an all-night truck stop along I-80 somewhere east of Omaha, Nebraska. It had rained most of the way from Cheyenne, and I was still twelve hours out of Greenfield. Saying I was exhausted didn't even scratch the surface of how I was feeling.

I was halfway through a plate of steak, eggs, hash browns, toast, and a side of fried apples when I heard the guy on the TV behind the counter talking about a young man in Laramie who had been tied to a fence, tortured, and left to die. His name was Matthew Shepherd, and the police thought he was attacked because he was gay. Maybe I was full of sadness about my mom dying, or perhaps I was just tired as hell, but hearing about that boy made my heart hurt, and I lost interest in my midnight breakfast. I asked for a refill on my coffee, grabbed a slice of toast off my plate, and went over to sit in a booth by the window.

As I was dipping my toast in my coffee, I got to thinking of the first time someone called me a queer.

◊ ◊ ◊ ◊ ◊ ◊ ◊ ◊ ◊ ◊ ◊ ◊ ◊ ◊ ◊ ◊ ◊ ◊ ◊

I was eight years old, and Mom had taken Maureen and me to the Cincinnati Zoo one Saturday morning. We were watching a black bear pace back and forth in his pen when I saw a man wearing a fedora and a silky purple shirt with an orange scarf tied around his neck walk up and stand beside us. For some reason, I thought that was the coolest thing I had ever seen. I mean the man in the orange scarf. Not the pacing bear. I wanted to have that same outfit for myself, so I pointed at him and asked my mom if she'd buy me a purple shirt and an orange thing to tie around my neck like that guy was wearing. Mom looked at him, then at me, then at him again, before saying, "You've got to be joking. I wouldn't let you dress like that for all the tea in China." Well, that wasn't the answer I was looking for, so the next day after church, I started going through my clothes, hoping to make an outfit like that guy at the zoo was wearing. The best I could come up with was a gray and white flannel shirt with thin purple lines and an orange and blue scarf from my mom's closet. It was a warm May Monday morning when I walked out of the house for school in my flannel shirt. If Mom noticed, she didn't mention it.

I waited until I was almost to school before taking the scarf from my pocket and tying it around my neck, the ends hanging in front of my right shoulder. I checked myself in the window of Steven's TV Repair, and I thought it looked fabulous. The other kids didn't think so, though. Most of them just pointed and laughed, but a group of older boys, smoking on the steps of the Presbyterian Church, called me a "fruitcake" and flicked their cigarette butts at me.

It was Buddy Murphy, though, who pushed me over the edge. When I was walking into our classroom, he shoved me in the back and said, "You look like a queer with that thing around your neck."

Now, I didn't know precisely what a queer was, but I had heard others say it enough that I knew it wasn't a good thing. So, I punched Buddy as hard as I could in the mouth, which caused him to cry and spit blood all over the floor. To top it off, I called him a "No good son of a bitch," and a "Goddamn white trash hillbilly." My teacher, Mrs. Coburn, didn't care for the blood on the floor, but she absolutely hated the words coming out of my mouth. So she grabbed me by the arm and hauled me to the principal's office, where Mr. Pike gave me three whacks with the paddle and told me to take that silly thing off my neck and to never use that kind of foul language again. He didn't even mention poor Buddy and his loose teeth.

Mom met me at the door when I got home from school that day. "Mr. Pike called this morning," she said as she commenced whipping me with a maple switch, demanding to know where I had learned such filthy language.

Thinking fast, I said, "I heard the older boys saying it on the way to school. I didn't know what it meant." Mom either didn't hear my explanation or didn't care, so she just kept whipping me and didn't let up until she was satisfied that I had learned my lesson.

The truth is, I learned to cuss and use course language from hanging around outside Daniels Pool Hall, where my uncle Robert was a hustler. Me and my cousins, Mike and Will, would wait for him to get done playing in the evening so we could walk home with him. He always had a pocket full of quarters and half dollars, and sometimes, he'd buy us a bottle of pop or a candy bar because he was in a good mood from winning. "Skinnin' them idiots," he called it. Any other time, he wouldn't buy us anything. Anyway, we heard him and the other men at the pool hall cuss and hurl insults at people on a regular basis. We were amazed by how eloquent some of them were. Uncle Robert was one of the best. At times, he was almost poetic. Younger guys who thought they could beat him playing pool were "piss ants." Guys who always hung around talking about how good they were but rarely played were "benchwarmers." He could spot queers, jungle bunnies, mackerel snappers, sluts, Hungarian refugees, city slickers, farm jakes, welfare trash, sissies, dumbasses, hillbillies, drunk bums, holy rollers, and

Republicans from a mile away. People behaving poorly were "Sick sons-a-bitches." People behaving stupidly were "dumb dumbs," "simpletons," or just "simps."

Uncle Robert didn't believe in using any words with sexual connotations, though, especially the F word. He said, "That's a dirty word and only trash and no good dirty rotten sons-a-bitches ever say it." To this day, thanks mainly to pious Uncle Robert, I never say the F word.

◊ ◊ ◊ ◊ ◊ ◊ ◊ ◊ ◊ ◊ ◊ ◊ ◊ ◊ ◊ ◊ ◊ ◊ ◊ ◊

I stared out the diner window into the dark and watched the rain coming down on the cars parked in the lot. Up on the interstate, I could see trucks driving by in both directions, delivering stuff to places that needed it, I guess. The scene gave me a lonely feeling and made me miss something, but I didn't know what.

The waitress filled my coffee cup, and I asked her where a good place to spend the night was. She said there was a Motel 6 just two exits down, so I finished my coffee, paid the check, and headed on my way.

Only three vehicles were in the Motel 6 parking lot when I pulled in and parked under a light near the front door. I was greeted by Elvis Presley singing "Burning Love" at full volume and a smell that I recognized as that stuff they used to soak up vomit off the floor in grade school.

Standing at the front desk, I filled my pockets with Lifesaver mints from a white bowl sitting next to a green bowl full of hard apples while I waited. Five minutes passed before a short, smartly dressed East Asian man emerged from a door marked EMPLOYEES ONLY. The plastic tag on his lapel told me his name was "Carl" and he was the Manager. He turned the music down and said, "Good evening, sir. I am very sorry for the odor of vomit. How can I help you?" in a voice that assured me his name was not really Carl.

"I need a room for one, please. Preferably far away from any other occupied room."

"Very well, sir," Carl replied.

After giving Carl all the pertinent information and my credit card, he handed me a key on a ring with the number 137.

"Thank you, sir," Carl said with a smile. "A continental breakfast is served in the lobby from six a.m. to nine a.m. The pool is closed, I'm afraid," he said with genuine regret. "Your room is on the left side, past the elevator. Near the end of the hall. I hope you enjoy your stay."

As I walked toward my room, I saw the source of the offensive odor and stepped over a mess in front of the elevator. When I went inside my room and closed the door, I was pleased that the smell did not accompany me.

I woke up at a quarter till six the next morning. After a hot shower, I grabbed a handful of mini muffins and a cup of coffee from the continental breakfast in the lobby, then jumped in my car and headed east.

◊ ◊ ◊ ◊ ◊ ◊ ◊ ◊ ◊ ◊ ◊ ◊ ◊ ◊ ◊ ◊ ◊ ◊ ◊ ◊

The muffins got me thinking about the sweets that my Sunday school teacher, Miss Judy Reemers, brought to class every Sunday when I was a kid. She always had homemade cookies, little cupcakes, or Bisquick donuts for us to eat while she taught us about Jesus, loving one another, and being nice to our neighbors. I have always made it a point to try to be nice to others even when they aren't nice to me. That philosophy has served me well over the years, and I thank Miss Judy for instilling it in me.

My mother was a Christian lady, and she took me and my sister to the First Baptist Church every Sunday morning and sometimes on Wednesday evenings. I remember sitting in the pews watching the preacher turn purple as he rallied the faithful against homosexuals, sodomites, and perverts. He would tremble and shake as the sweat poured from his forehead, and I would look around at all the faces and wonder if any of those people were homosexuals or maybe even sodomites or perverts. I wondered how easy it was to spot one since I didn't even know what one was. Strangely, the preacher never went after liars, cheats, deadbeats, drunkards, hypocrites, or even murderers with anything remotely close to the same vigor. It seemed to me that being a sodomite was just about the worst thing a person could be, but I wasn't sure why, and I never heard anyone ask.

Around noon, I made it to St. Louis and stopped for gas. I wasn't hungry, but I grabbed a cup of coffee from a Dunkin Donuts and pulled off into a little park near the exit. There was a blacktop path that made a loop around the outside of the park, so I decided to take a walk while I drank my coffee.

It was my Freshman year of high school when I started figuring out I was probably gay. I tried to like Michelle Phillips, Marlo Thomas, and Sally Fields but couldn't see the appeal. I was more interested in Davy Jones and Paul McCartney. The same with the prettiest girls at school: Jenny Rogers, Barbie Blanton, Sarah Heslep, Robin Bishop... None of them caused the same stir inside me as they obviously did the other guys. The realization caused me a lot of anxiety, and I tried everything I could to prove I wasn't gay. I gazed at pretty girls at every opportunity, trying to see what was so great about them. I borrowed some of Uncle Robert's Playboy magazines from Mike and Will and looked at them for hours on end. I even asked Jenny Rogers out on a date (she declined immediately). None of these things helped.

Around the same time, the rumor that I was gay started to make the rounds. I don't think anyone really believed I was gay. We were just at that age where kids would look for any reason to attack other kids, and that was what they came up with. I didn't act, talk, or walk like the stereotypical gay male. I played sports, got in my share of fights, hunted, fished, smoked cigarettes, and did everything else the other guys in my neighborhood did other than obsess over girls. The problem was my clothes. I liked colorful button-down shirts with big collars and bell bottoms. Sometimes, I wore beads around my neck and sunglasses with orange lenses. In short, I was a few years ahead of the trend in southern Ohio. Had it been 1970 instead of 1966, people would have said I dressed like Sonny Bono.

When I got back to my car, I started thinking of that Sheppard boy again and wondered what he must have done to deserve what he got. He probably smiled at the wrong guy, or maybe his lisp was too pronounced. Perhaps he just dressed funny.

◊ ◊ ◊ ◊ ◊ ◊ ◊ ◊ ◊ ◊ ◊ ◊ ◊ ◊ ◊ ◊ ◊ ◊ ◊ ◊

Pulling back onto the interstate, the song "White Rabbit" by The Jefferson Airplane came on the radio. That took me back to 1967 when I was a junior in high school and went on the second date I had ever gone on. (The first one was with Laura Ann Lovejoy at the junior high Spring dance when I was fourteen. Our mothers had arranged it, and Laura and I had a miserable time.) Anyway, my second date was with Jimmy Simon, who was also a Junior at McClain High School. Remember, it was 1967, so we weren't advertising that we were on a date. In fact, I went to great lengths to ensure that no one knew Jimmy and I were together at all. One evening, I drove my mom's car, taking the side streets to Jimmy's house, and picked him up. Then we went to the Ranch Drive Inn to see "Bonnie and Clyde." I made Jimmy lay on the back floorboard with a blanket over himself as I drove through the gate. Then we parked way up front and to the far right, widely considered the worst place to watch a movie from, to reduce the risk of anyone spotting us. Jimmy even brought a couple bottles of Pepsi and a bag of potato chips, so we didn't need to go to the concession stand. Maybe I should mention that Jimmy was very effeminate, and there was no doubt in anyone's mind that he was gay. So, getting seen together would have been all the proof anyone needed that I was also gay.

At one point, I started to hold Jimmy's hand during the movie but couldn't get up the nerve to do it. However, during the scene when Blanche Barrow went berserk during the shootout, something came over Jimmy, and he cuddled up next to me, leaned over, and kissed me right on the mouth. I won't go into details, but suffice it to say that we didn't watch any more of the movie.

The next day, I took the side streets to Jimmy's house again and picked him up so we could drive to Washington Court House for a burger and shake at Dairy Queen. That turned out to be a mistake. A group of boys, teenagers about our age, watched us get out of the car and announced, "Here come a couple of Greenfield hillbillies. Hold your noses." I'm unsure how they knew we were from Greenfield, but they may have spotted the small Tiger Band Boosters sticker on our car's rear bumper. Regardless, they knew.

Jimmy and I got our food, and instead of just taking it back to the car and leaving, we decided to sit at one of the picnic tables and eat there. We heard the boys talking and laughing, probably at us, but they weren't really bothering us. Yet. When we got up to leave, one of the boys wadded up a paper cup and threw it our way. The cup hit me right on the end of the nose. Now, it didn't hurt as much as it pissed me off. Remember, I grew up on the south end of Greenfield. No one was going to hit me with anything and not suffer some kind of retribution. So, I picked up the cup off the ground, walked to the boy who threw it, and gently dropped it right in the middle of the banana split he was eating.

That didn't go over so well. When the boy stood up, I saw he was a foot taller than me and outweighed me by thirty pounds at least. He didn't hesitate, taking a swing that grazed my right cheek as I stepped back and threw a counter punch that connected with his lower lip, busting it open. What happened next was typical bully behavior. Instead of coming after me, he simply stopped. He wiped the blood from his lip with a napkin, looked around at his friends who were expecting him to pulverize me, and mumbled something about kicking my ass the next time he saw me. You see, bullies don't like it when you fight back.

What happened next was a game changer. Jimmy, who was probably the gayest acting guy I have ever known, committed one of the gayest acts I have witnessed to this day; he stuck his tongue out at these guys and actually said, "Nah, nah, nah, nah, nah!" Then he wrapped his arms around my neck and kissed me right on the cheek. That might as well have been the kiss of death.

"They're fucking faggots." The big guy said it in the same voice he may have used to announce that we were fucking aliens or fucking werewolves or fucking leprechauns. It was like he couldn't believe that he was seeing a pair of living, breathing fucking faggots right before his very eyes.

I've heard people say that their blood ran cold when they were very frightened by something. Well, I'm not ashamed to say that my blood ran cold at that moment. My biggest secret was exposed. I was now an identifiable member of one of the most secretive, marginalized, taboo segments of southern Ohio Appalachian culture, and my identifiers didn't appear to be in a tolerant mood at that very moment.

Jimmy absorbed the first shot. One of the guys gave him an open-handed slap to the side of the head, and Jimmy hit the ground, curled up in a ball, and cried.

I took the second shot from someone behind me, who hit me in the back of the head. Not hard, but enough to knock me forward. My reaction was swift, and I punched the big guy in front of me as hard as I could in the mouth again. That surprised him, and before he could react, I hit him for the third time in less than a minute, this time in the throat. That one seemed to wake him up a little, and he grabbed me by the shirt with both hands and slung me to the ground next to Jimmy. At that point, the whole bunch commenced stomping Jimmy and me into the ground.

I still recall how the gravel felt against my face and tasting the dust in my mouth that mixed with blood and formed a paste that I thought would choke me. I heard Jimmy crying and begging them to stop, and that really hurt me. It still hurts me today to think about it.

The last thing I remember before losing consciousness was a girl's voice. She said, "Kill those queers!" Maybe it was the girl who made our milkshakes. I'm not sure.

When I woke up, I was lying flat on my back next to Jimmy. Two women were kneeling down beside us. One was a black woman of about fifty with thick glasses that made her eyes look huge. The other was a white woman in her early thirties with a cigarette dangling from her lips.

"Oh, thank you, Jesus!" the black woman said when she realized I was alive.

The white woman asked me if I was okay, and I responded that I was not, in fact, okay. She told me an ambulance was coming, and everything would be fine. I'm not sure I believed her.

Jimmy wasn't moving, and his face was covered in blood. I tried to get up and see if I could help him, but the two women told me not to move.

"Is he dead," I asked. Afraid to hear the answer.

"No," the black woman answered. "He's been moving around a little."

"Here comes the ambulance," the white woman said.

I saw what looked like a hearse pull into the lot, and I thought maybe I was dead after all. A couple seconds later, a police cruiser pulled in as well.

The two women started to depart, but before they did, the white woman leaned close to me and said in a low voice, "My nephew is funny like you, so I know how hard it is. I feel sorry for you and hope you're able to change someday. Until then, please be careful and don't get hurt again. I don't pray much, but I will pray for you and your boyfriend."

"He's not my boyfriend. I'm not gay," I said. "We're just friends."

"Oh, okay," the woman said with a smirk. "I better pray anyway. Just in case." Then she patted my arm gently and went to join the rest of the gawkers watching from the sidewalk.

Jimmy was loaded into the ambulance, and I was placed in the back of the police cruiser for the four-minute trip to the hospital.

I was kept overnight for observation and discharged the next day. I had a possible concussion, two broken fingers (probably from punching the big boy so many times), and I needed twelve stitches in my head, on top of being bruised from head to toe.

Jimmy was transferred to Ohio State Medical Center and underwent surgery to remove his ruptured spleen. His left eardrum was severely damaged, and he lost hearing in that ear. He was also covered with bruises over most of his body and needed three stitches above his right eye and seven in his lower lip.

The boys who assaulted us were never arrested. The police said there were no witnesses, although I knew there were at least five. Probably more.

I was out of school for a week, and Jimmy never returned.

I lost a lot of friends. Clint Walker said his dad wouldn't let him hang around a dick sucker. Bobby Benton sent word through his little sister that he would kill me if I ever came around him again. I did, and he didn't. My cousins, Mike and Will, said they always wondered if I was a peter puffer but didn't really seem to be that upset. Although they sometimes avoided me in public, especially if many other boys were around. Uncle Robert told me that he couldn't understand what I found attractive in a man's hairy ass, but as long as I didn't act like a fairy around him, I could stick my hoo-dinker wherever the hell I pleased on my own time. Aunt Helen asked me what was wrong with me but treated me as good as ever.

The verbal abuse I suffered in the hallway for the rest of that school year was pretty brutal. But at least it never got physical. My swimming teacher, Mr. Wiley, informed me he couldn't have a homosexual hanging around the locker room, so he threw me out of his class and gave me an Incomplete.

My mother only mentioned my sexual orientation one time. A couple days after I came home from the hospital, I was sitting in the backyard sulking, and she sat down beside me. "Morris," she said, "I have known since you were a little boy. I just had a feeling. A mother's intuition, maybe. I won't lie; I wish you weren't a homosexual. Simply because life would be easier on you if you weren't. But you're my son, and no strings are attached to my love for you. I will always be your mother and always be on your side." Then she got up and walked into the house.

That simple declaration of love from my mother probably saved my life. I'm not sure I would be here today had she not told me she loved me unconditionally. I'll never forget it, and I will always cherish her memory.

Mom paid a price for loving me so. She lost lifelong friends and sometimes got a chilly reception when she went shopping or uptown for lunch. She stopped going to church after a few weeks. I'm unsure if a "sodomite sermon" drove her off or if she just felt uncomfortable being there. She never talked about it. She didn't go back for three years; she just read her bible, prayed, and worshiped with Billy Graham on the radio. One Sunday morning, though, she got up and went back. Just walked in like she'd never been gone and picked up where she left off. Mom loved God, and God loved her back. I was happy for her.

When Jimmy left the hospital, his parents sent him to live with his grandparents in New Philadelphia to finish high school. I only saw him one time after that. I ran into him and his father in Dixon's Grocery when he was home for Christmas. I said hello, and Jimmy smiled, but his father pushed him along and made it clear that Jimmy wouldn't be talking to me. I heard Jimmy tried to join the Army after high school but was rejected due to his hearing loss. After that, he went to community college for a semester, dropped out, and got a job delivering pizzas. At some point, Jimmy discovered LSD and heroin. On December 31, 1970, he jumped from the top of a water tower in Youngstown and ended his life. He was twenty years old.

◊ ◊ ◊ ◊ ◊ ◊ ◊ ◊ ◊ ◊ ◊ ◊ ◊ ◊ ◊ ◊ ◊ ◊ ◊

I don't know how many laps I walked around that park, but it was time to get on the road. The weather was excellent, and I was making good time, so I considered driving all the way to Greenfield, but that would have put me in town around ten o'clock, and I knew Maureen went to bed early. So, after consulting my map, I decided to shoot for Louisville, KY, instead.

Interstate 64 between St. Louis and Louisville is almost barren. Only Evansville breaks up the blandness; if you've ever been to Evansville, you know that's not saying much.

◊ ◊ ◊ ◊ ◊ ◊ ◊ ◊ ◊ ◊ ◊ ◊ ◊ ◊ ◊ ◊ ◊ ◊ ◊ ◊

It got me thinking that the first time I ever traveled this road, albeit going west, not east. It was 1969, just nine days after I graduated from high school. I got on a bus in Chillicothe and took it all the way to San Diego to spend the summer with my sister, Maureen, and her husband, Tom, who was in the Navy. That was my first trip out of Ohio. Along the way, I saw the Mississippi River, the St. Louis Arch, the world's largest ball of twine, three grizzly bears, the Grand Canyon, and an ancient Indian who claimed to be General George Armstrong Custer's half-breed son. I don't think he really was, but I paid him a dollar for an autographed photo anyway. He signed it "Long Fish Custer." I also ate supper in a diner in Osawatomie, Kansas, where Richard Nixon had a slice of apple pie and a cup of coffee while campaigning for President in 1960. There was a picture on the wall next to the restroom door to prove it lest anyone doubt it was true.

San Diego was worlds away from Greenfield. A west coast city of half a million was almost more than a boy from a Midwest town of five thousand could handle. Maureen, who was aware of my unintentional coming out but never mentioned it, took me all over. We went to Old San Diego, where I had a taco for the first time. We spent hours walking around Balboa Park, visiting the museums, going to movies, and eating ice cream. We made several trips to the San Diego Zoo and even went to a San Diego Padres game.

Ocean Beach was the real eye-opener, though. OB was called the Haight-Ashbury District of San Diego, and for good reason. I'd seen hippies on TV, and there were a couple guys and girls in Greenfield who pretended to be hippies, but Ocean Beach was hippie central as far as I was concerned. They were everywhere. And you know what? They weren't bothering anybody. They played music, smoked weed, danced on the street corners, gave flowers to strangers, and lay on the beach soaking up the sun.

I smoked marijuana for the first time with a handsome Gunner's Mate from the USS Andrew Johnson one night on the beach. We saw each other a few times over the next two weeks, then he sailed for Hawaii, and that was that.

Nothing in my nineteen years on Earth prepared me to see openly gay and lesbian couples in public like I saw in San Diego. There weren't a lot of them, and they weren't everywhere, mainly confining themselves to Ocean Beach and areas of downtown, but there were enough that it didn't seem odd after a couple weeks. That was life-changing, and for the first time since that day at Dairy Queen, I felt somewhat optimistic about the future.

The day after Labor Day, I boarded a bus to return home. I can't tell you how bad I wanted to stay in San Diego, but I had a midnight shift job waiting for me at the slaughterhouse, shooting rats and operating the bone grinder. It wasn't the most fabulous job in town, but it was the best I could do under the circumstances. Uncle Robert pulled a few strings with the personnel manager and the night shift foreman, both of whom owed him gambling debts, and got me hired on at $1.28 per hour.

A few weeks after coming home, I was walking the two blocks to work one evening, and a car sped by me as I passed Uncle Robert's and Aunt Helen's house. They slowed down, then made a U-turn at the train tracks and came back. I kept walking as the car pulled alongside me, and the driver rolled his window down. There were three guys in the car, and they were all wearing ski masks.

"Hey faggot," the driver said. "What are you doing out so late?

Before I could respond, I heard a familiar voice behind me. "Hi, Morris. Taking your late-night stroll?"

I turned and saw Uncle Robert walking off his porch, smoking a cigarette and carrying a baseball bat over his right shoulder.

"Uh, hi, Uncle Robert," I stammered. "I'm, uh, headed to work."

Uncle Robert turned his attention to the three masked men in the car. "What the hell are you three dumbasses doin'? Goin' bobsleddin'? Robbin' a train? Trick or treatin'?"

"Mind your business, old man," the driver shot back.

"Old man? I'm thirty-seven!"

The driver started to open his door, but Uncle Robert brought the bat off his shoulder, and the masked man thought better of it.

"Listen to me, piss ant. You and your little henchman get your light asses outta here before I lose my temper."

"Mister, there's three of us. I'm counting one of you plus a girl. We'll take our chances."

The driver opened his door, but I kicked it shut before he could get out. The two henchmen never moved. Uncle Robert smashed the windshield with his bat, and the driver yelled, "You smashed my windshield!"

With that, Uncle Robert drew the back bat and knocked the mirror off the door. "I knocked your mirror off too, asshole. Next, I'm gonna bash your skull in."

"You ain't heard the last of this!" The driver snarled as

he threw his car into Drive and sped away.

"I hope not!" Uncle Robert yelled after him. Hell, I'd like to do this again!"

At that moment, it became clear that my future was not in Greenfield.

That night at work, while grinding bones and shooting rats, I decided that it would be best if I started my life over somewhere else. So, the next morning, when I got home from work, I told my mother what I planned to do. She was heartbroken, but she understood that being a gay man in Greenfield, Ohio, was not going to be easy. She knew I needed a fresh start

"Where will you go, Morris?" she asked. "Back to San Diego?"

The thought had crossed my mind, but I was afraid that I wouldn't survive there. Embracing the free-loving hippie culture scared me some, and I decided things probably wouldn't end well.

A National Geographic magazine was lying on the coffee table. I picked it up and flipped to a map of the United States, then I closed my eyes and jabbed my finger into the page. When I opened my eyes, I saw where my finger pointed. "Mom. I'm going to Cheyenne, Wyoming."

Planning my move began right away. First and foremost, if I was going to get out of Greenfield, I needed a car. To buy a car, I needed money. My savings account at The People's National Bank had twenty-seven dollars and thirty-three cents, and the Maxwell House can in my bedroom contained four dollars and ninety-one cents. That was the extent of my liquid assets. So, I decided my best option was to continue working at the slaughterhouse and doing odd jobs until I had enough money to buy a reliable car. I set my sights on April 1,

1970, just under six months away.

The next several months weren't easy. I took all the overtime I could get at the slaughterhouse, did as many odd jobs around the neighborhood as possible, and picked up a weekend job unloading trucks at Dixon's Grocery. I hated the job at Dixon's. The owner, Harold Dixon, hired me on one condition: that I not be anywhere around the store thirty minutes before opening to thirty minutes after closing because he didn't want his customers to see me. "Listen," he said. "I really don't have anything against you people, myself. My customers might be a little uncomfortable, though. It's already bad enough that I have that colored boy working here. Adding a, uh, fag... er, uh, I mean homosexual might be too much. You understand, right?" Well, I didn't understand, but I didn't say anything because I needed money.

By March 15, I had managed to save almost nine hundred dollars. The first thing I did was quit at Dixon's without notice. After clocking out for the last time, I went to the restroom, stuffed two rolls of toilet paper as far down the toilet as possible, and flushed it six times before leaving. It was a tiny act of retribution, but it was the best I could come up with at the moment. That evening, I went to work at the slaughterhouse and gave my two weeks' notice. Working there wasn't always pleasant, but I can't say I was mistreated. Sure, I got harassed a little at first, but after a couple weeks, it let up, and I was just another one of the guys. After I finished my last shift, the fellas used a permanent marker to write "MORRIS DELANEY. TOP RAT KILLER ACE. 43 CONFIRMED KILLS." on the wall behind the bone grinder. They also drew two crossed penises with the initials "MLD" underneath for good measure. Then we went out to the parking lot and had a beer. I was honored.

◊ ◊

It was a little past five o'clock when I got to Louisville, and I was exhausted. I got a room at a Knights Inn, bought a sandwich from a vending machine, and hit the sack.

I got up early the next morning, anxious to get on the road and get to Greenfield before lunch. Walking to my car, I looked across the parking lot and noticed a Waffle House next to the hotel. The place wasn't busy, and I sat in a booth by the window. The waitress, a middle-aged woman named Florence, greeted me with a mostly toothless smile, then filled my cup with surprisingly good coffee and took my order. Two waffles, two scrambled eggs, and two sausage links.

◊ ◊

As I sipped my coffee and waited for my breakfast, I thought back to March 28, 1970, three days before I left for Cheyenne.

I had bought a 1964 Chevy Impala for six hundred thirty-five dollars. It was clean and ran well, and I asked Uncle Robert to look at it and help me prepare it for its cross-country trip. He changed the plugs and air filter for me, and I went to the junkyard and bought a jack to replace the broken one in the boot. Finally, I gave it a good washing and waxing, and Uncle Robert said, "Well, it'll get you to Wyoming as long as you drive it like you have some sense."

Word had gotten around town that I was leaving, and

two people had asked to make the trip with me: Delbert Greene, a kid a couple years younger than me who had quit school after the ninth grade, and a guy wearing a leg brace, sweating profusely, and smelling like an outhouse named Dwight Kessler. I turned down both offers, though. Delbert, because he was only sixteen years old and I didn't want the liability, and Dwight, because he smelled like an outhouse. Plus, why would I want to take two people from Greenfield to start a new life elsewhere?

The day before I was to leave for Cheyenne, I was sitting on the front porch with Mom, and a motorcycle pulled up in front of the house. A girl I knew only as Pearl hopped off the back, and the motorcycle sped away. Pearl walked up to me and said, "I heard you're going to Wyoming. I want to go with you. My aunt lives in Hollywood, and I'm going out to stay with her for a while. I can take a bus to Hollywood if you'll take me to Cheyenne. I have a hundred dollars for gas and food."

Pearl was two years older than me and three years ahead of me in school. I remembered her as a dorky-looking girl with braces and black-framed glasses, but she had blossomed since I saw her last. She was beautiful. Even a gay boy like me could tell that. She was tall, rather voluptuous, with long legs, green eyes, and bleach-blonde hair. She was dressed in bell bottoms, sandals, and a loose white shirt with a wide leather belt keeping it closed. She wore sunglasses, beads around her neck, and flowers in her hair. She was obviously not wearing a bra. Honestly, I was jealous of her outfit.

"Well," I said. "I reckon that'll be just fine."

Part 2 of "Morris Delaney Ain't No Sissy" will be released in 2024. Don't miss it!

STRAIGHT OUTTA GREENFIELD

PART ONE

Booty Wilson parked across the street from Pearl's Coffeehouse and cracked his window. He picked up the pack of smokes from the dash, took the last one out, and threw the empty pack on the floorboard alongside an assortment of fast-food wrappers, empty bottles and cans, rolled up boogers, and bits of fingernail. He felt his pockets for a lighter, came up empty handed, then rummaged through the glove box until he found a book of matches from Dusty's Cabaret in Troy, Missouri, and lit his smoke. It was ten thirty-one am.

A light rain had fallen most of the morning. The sky was gray with no hint of sunshine, and there was a chill in the air. Typical for mid-November. It was the kind of weather that Booty hated, and it was the driving force behind his ongoing efforts to scrape together enough money to buy a decent vehicle and move to Florida, where his mom and stepdad manage The Sandy Turtle Mobile Home Park in Fort Pierce. Booty smiled, thinking of himself kicked back by the tenant's pool with a cooler full of beer; lying in the sun and chatting up the young baby mommas. But work, the good-paying kind, had been scarce the last few months, and he lacked the funds to travel south. Booty Wilson needed a big pay day.

Suddenly, a white van with a busted exhaust pulled into the parking space in front of him. Booty watched his stepbrother, Dickey Dance, exit the passenger side door, run across the street on his toes, dodging puddles, and into the coffeehouse.

Booty laughed to himself as warm air from the vents caused the stale farts in his stained seats to permeate the air and mix with the sound of the windshield wipers pushing water from the glass. Booty's eyes became heavy, and he felt himself drifting off to sleep. So, he snuffed out his cigarette in the ashtray, rolled up his window, reclined his seat, and began snoring.

The slam of a car door jolted Booty awake, causing him to sit straight up in his seat. In the rearview mirror, Booty watched a thin man exit the red Honda Accord and walk towards the entrance of the coffeehouse. It was Tom Allen. Booty checked his watch. Ten fifty - nine a.m. Time to go to work.

When Booty walked in, Tom was sitting in his usual spot, the booth in the corner farthest from the door, and Dickey sat at the counter chatting up the young blonde barista, who was noticeably disinterested.

As Bootie hurried past the counter, he snapped his fingers at Dickey, and they both made their way across the room to join Tom.

"Well, look who it is. Booty Wilson and The Dick Dance Kid," Tom Allen said with a smirk. "Sit down, boys."

Booty and Dickey sat down in the booth and glanced

around nervously.

"Morning, guys," Pearl King said with a smile. What can I get ya?"

"Good morning, Pearl," Tom said. Just coffee. Black."

Pearl looked at Booty. "How about you, hun?"

"Decaf. With oat milk," Booty replied.

Tom chuckled.

"I'm lactose intolerant," Booty shrugged.

"And for you, Dickey?" Pearl asked.

"I'll have a large Americano with four cream and six sugars. And an apple cinnamon scone. Warmed up, please."

"Is this all on one check?" Pearl asked.

Booty and Dickey pretended not to hear the question.

"Separate checks," Tom answered.

"I'll have it right out."

Booty saw Tom watching Pearl walk away and thought it odd that he would be so interested in a woman well into her late fifties and dumpy in the ass. Booty was too young to know that Pearl Davis was the most beautiful woman in Greenfield thirty years ago. Tom Allen, on the other hand, remembered it fondly.

It had been a few months since Tom had called on Booty and Dickey about a job. That wasn't necessarily out of the ordinary, but it always gave Booty pause anyway. In the back of his mind, he wondered if Tom had lost confidence in him.

Booty and Tom were not friends in any sense of the word. They didn't socialize or exchange Christmas cards. Nor did they call to see how the other was doing. They were business associates and uneasy ones at that. Two men existing in the same spinning circle but at different points within. Tom was firmly planted in the stable center while Booty hung on nervously along the volatile edge, always in danger of being tossed out.

Tom was a Greenfield native and had a lovely two-story stone house with a pool and three-car garage on Franklin Drive. However, he spent most of his time in a swanky apartment high in the sky in downtown Columbus, where he could keep tabs on his upscale gentlemen's club, Super Daddy's.

In addition to running Columbus' number one strip joint, Tom was the kingpin of Greenfield's shadowy underworld of corruption and vice, which now consisted primarily of keeping tweakers and dope fiends supplied with pills and rock, fencing stolen goods, and a card game that Bob Connor ran on Saturday nights for Greenfield's more senior hustlers. Nothing like the bad old days that stretched from the end of World War One through Jerry Garner's downfall in 1987. Back then, Greenfield was known as Little Chicago. Illegal booze, marijuana, cocaine, prostitution, gambling, gun running, and loan sharking were rampant. There were an equal number of beer joints and churches in town, giving folks ample opportunity to repent on Sunday morning for the hell they had raised on Saturday night.

Booty, on the other hand, shared a rundown rental with Dickey across the Tenth Street bridge in Higginsville. He was employed part-time at Hartman's Junkyard and seasonally at Early Bird's Greenhouse.

When Tom reached out to Booty (it was never the other way around), it meant that Tom stood to make a lot of money by using his connections, and Booty stood to get a decent cut by using his willingness to assume risk.

Booty glanced around the cafe. Besides himself, Tom, Dickey, Pearl, and the young girl behind the counter, a teenage boy was trying to look busy running a broom over the same spot on the wood floor. Two old men sat, drinking coffee and reading the paper, at a table by the door, and a sad-looking middle-aged woman was at the counter whispering to herself, eating a donut, and drinking a glass of orange juice through a straw. Quiet for a Saturday morning, Booty thought.

"So, how ya been, Booty?" Tom said. "It's been a while. Six, eight months, maybe."

"I've been doing okay. Working a lot at the junkyard. Been thinking about mo..."

"Would you look at that? She ain't wearing a bra," Dickey whispered, nodding toward a teenage girl who had just walked in the door and stood ordering at the counter. Those gotta be 36 Cs easy."

Tom turned to look at the girl. "Come on, man. What is she, fifteen? She's wearing a retainer."

"Nah, I bet she's sixteen at least, maybe even seventeen. Seventeen and a half," Dickey answered.

"That's jailbait, Dickey. You have tee shirts older than those tits," Booty offered.

Dickey shook his head. "See, that's what I'm always talkin' about, man. You are a perpetual downer. Always goin' south. Live a little, buddy. Go north sometimes!"

"Kiss my ass," Booty said as Dickey grinned and slapped him on the back.

Tom groaned. "Just shut the fuck up. We got a lot to discuss, and we don't have all day to do it."

Dickey feigned disappointment and put both hands in the air. "You got it, Cap'n. I'm all business. Tell old Dickey what's on your mind."

Dickey had lived in Greenfield all his life except for a stint in the Army during the Iraq War. He had been an exceptional athlete in high school, earning All-South Central Ohio League honors in basketball during his junior and senior seasons. Still, he was a terrible student, and it took a lot of creative grading to keep Dickey eligible to play.

After his Army stint, Dickey had settled into a routine of finding ways to get by instead of working full-time. Odd jobs here and there: mowing yards, digging post holes, hauling trash, painting fences. He also sold drugs, mostly marijuana, stole tools from construction sites, and helped Booty whenever Tom Allen called.

"Here you go, guys." Pearl set a tray on the table. "Black for you. Decaf with oat milk for you. And an Americano with cream and sugar, and an apple cinnamon scone for you. Anything else I can get you?"

"That's it, darlin'. Thank you," Tom answered.

As Pearl walked away, Dickey started to say something, but Tom reached out and touched his arm. "Leave it."

"I was going to ask for some butter for my scone," Dickey protested.

"Let's move on," Tom said sternly, looking at Dickey.

"The floor is yours, Cap'n," Dickey said.

"I need someone to make a roundtrip run."

"We're listening," Booty said.

"My nephew, Phil...."

"Phil the Pill? Is he out?" Booty asked.

"Yeah. Got out of Ross Correctional six weeks ago. He's keeping a low profile down in Kentucky. Living with his sister in some little shithole south of Lexington that I've never heard of." Tom pulled a piece of paper from his shirt pocket, held it at arm's length, and looked at it with squinted eyes. "Junction City. It's an hour below Lexington. I'm sending him a little product to help him get back in business. Sort of a welcome home present."

Booty glanced around the cafe. "What kind of product?"

"Oxycodone mostly."

"Hillbilly Heroin," Dickey whispered, pouring the last of six packets of sugar into his coffee and stirring it with a plastic spoon.

"Weed. A little morphine. "

"Okay," Booty said. "That sounds simple enough. You said it's a round trip. I'm guessing we're bringing something back to Greenfield."

"Everything okay, guys?" Pearl asked, approaching the table. "You all need anything?"

"No, we're good, Pearl. Thanks, darlin'," Tom answered.

"Can I get a cheese Danish, please?" Dickey said before Pearl walked away.

"Sure thing, Dickey. I'll bring it right out."

Booty shook his head.

"Godammit, Dickey," Tom said. "You're like a fuckin' kid."

"Cap'n, I'm sorry, but I'm hungry. I ain't ate…"

"For crying out loud, shut the fuck up. And if you call me "Cap'n" again…"

"Here's your Danish, sweetie," Pearl said, setting a plate down before Dickie.

"Thanks, Pearl," Dickey answered while smirking at Tom.

"Anyway, Tom, what are we bringing back?" Booty asked.

Tom waited until Pearl was out of earshot. "A big load of H. Enough to keep us going for six months. Plus, some top-shelf marijuana. Maybe a little coke."

"Why ain't it just coming down in the trunk of a car from Detroit, like usual?" Booty asked.

Tom leaned in close. "Phil met a couple guys inside that are connected to some big players south of the border. One of which collapsed in the yard a few months ago from a massive heart attack. Phil saw him go down and gave him CPR. Saved the guy's life. The guy's Uncle is Costelo Garcia. Second in command of the Dominguez Cartel. He's showing his gratitude to Phil by making a one-time direct delivery to us. Bypassing the Detroit distributors and putting more money in our pockets. This is premium shit coming in. Plus we're getting it at a fifty percent discount. It's too much for Phil to manage, though. He doesn't have the experience, plus he has a nosy parole officer snoopin' around all the time. So I'm bringin' it up here."

"What's Detroit think about this?" Booty asked.

"I'm sure they don't like it. We'll worry about that when the time comes," Tom said with a shrug.

Dickey grinned. "This is some Sopranos-level shit."

"What's in this for us," Booty asked, nodding at Dickey.

"Three thousand dollars," Tom answered. Half when you leave. Half when you get back.

"Yeah, buddy!" Dickey slapped his hands together and smiled. "When do we leave?"

"Tomorrow morning," said Tom.

"Damn, not much time to prepare," Booty said.

"Things happened quickly."

"Okay. We'll make it work. Won't we, Dickey?"

"We sure as hell will," Dickey replied with a grin.

Tom nodded. "That's why I called you guys. I know I can count on you."

Booty and Dickey smiled and sat up straighter, buoyed by the compliment.

"Tomorrow morning, drive to Greenfield Textiles and park your car in the back of the parking lot. Leave the keys in it and get in the truck with the "Ed and Son

Electric" signs. The keys will be in the glove box. Drive the truck to Save-A-Lot and park next to the blue Mercedes near the center of the lot. It'll have its parking lights on. A man will get in the truck with you and give you your instructions. His name is Terrence." If you're not there by seven twenty, Terrence is driving away, and we're fucked. Got it?"

Booty looked at Dickey and nodded. Dickey nodded back. "Got it," they said in unison.

"Look, you two," Tom said, pointing his finger at Booty and Dickey. "I just need you to deliver my package to Phil and bring back the stuff from the Mexicans. That's it. Nothing else. No drama, no games, no surprises. Most of all, no going Greenfield on anyone's ass. Just drive down to Kentucky and back. Can you do it?"

"We can do it, boss," Booty said assuredly.

PART TWO

Thirty-year-old Wilbur Eugene "Booty" Wilson and twenty-nine-year-old Richard Nelson "Dickey" Dance were not only business associates; they were best friends and stepbrothers.

When Booty was five months old, his dad went to work one morning and never came home. Two months later, his mom got an envelope in the mail with two hundred dollars and a note that said, "You and the kid are better off without me." The letter was postmarked Horatio, Arkansas. It was the last anyone in Greenfield ever heard of Booty Wilson's dad.

Dickey's mom died in a car wreck on Route 41 when Dickey was three years old. She was on her way home from Washington Court House and slammed into the back of a dump truck that had stopped in the road just past the Wilson School. Her funeral was a closed-casket affair, owing primarily to her severed head.

Booty's mom and Dickey's dad met in the McClain High School principal's office one afternoon thanks to Booty, Dickey, and a bag of firecrackers, in May of 1996. They married six months later when Booty was sixteen and Dickey was fifteen. Except for Dickey's three-year enlistment in the Army, his seven-month marriage to Annie Benton, and Booty's eighteen-month tour of the Ohio Prison System, they had not spent more than a few days apart at any one time since.

Booty and Dickey were in the front room of their house on Budd Street. Booty sat in the ragged lawn chair by the stove reading the Daily Times, and Dickey drank beer and watched "Wheel Of Fortune" from the couch.

"Fuck me to tears," Booty said. "Elaine Sommers got married."

"To who?" Dickey asked. "My gawd, she's uglier than homemade sin."

"Some sorry fuck from Lynchburg. Sandy Duff."

"A man named Sandy? What the fuck?"

Booty made a face. "I remember when she was born. She was the ugliest baby I ever saw. Fat, bald, and bug-eyed."

"I remember, Dickey agreed. She looked like Uncle Fuckin' Fester."

"Well, I'll be damned," Booty said, looking over the top of his newspaper.

"What?"

"Emo Gotlieb died. Eighty-one years old."

"No shit? I remember Elmo. Had them numbers tattooed on his arm," replied Dickey.

"Emo. Not Elmo. Fuckin' dirty-ass German Nazis put him and his family in a death camp cause they was Jews. Emo was the only one that made it out."

Dickey popped the top on a can of PBR. "When we was kids, we used to follow him around town."

"All over town. Couldn't understand a word he said. Had that Polak accent. He was always good to us, though."

"That he was," Dickey agreed. "He was a good old Jew. Here's to Elmo," he said, toasting the ceiling and taking a swig of beer.

"Emo," Booty said."

"May he rest in peace," Dickey said solemnly. "Wait. Do Jews go to Heaven?"

"Hell yes, Jews go to Heaven. Jesus was a Jew."

Dickey looked surprised. "I thought Jesus was a Baptist."

"You're thinkin' of his brother, John."

"That's right," Dickie exclaimed, slapping his knee. "John. King of the Baptists!"

Booty turned his attention back to the paper. "Let's see who's been breakin' the law," he said, perusing the police blotter. "Looks like all the regulars. David Tuttle, public indecency."

"I heard about that. He was takin' a piss on the post office steps. Drunker 'n hell. Who else?"

"Ted Morrow. Litterin'."

"Ted Morrow? Our old neighbor?" Dickey asked.

"Yep. That's him."

"Hmph. Litterin'? They need to put his ass away."

They both laughed.

Booty continued, "Dwight Kessler. Shopliftin'."

"Don't know him."

"Donnie's uncle. Wears that shoe with a real thick sole."

"His name's Dwight? I always know'd him as Gimpy. I wish it said what he stole," Dickie remarked.

"Listen to this. Myron Tucker. Invasion Of Privacy. Peeping."

"That pervy bastard."

Booty thought for a second. "I hope it didn't require much walkin' around. He's handicapped as hell. Sucks on an oxygen tank 24/7. Always ridin' that scooter around Sav-A-Lot."

"Shit," Dickey snorted. "His only handicap is bein' a fat ass."

Booty grinned. "Here's one for you. Lester Slade."

"Lester Slade! What the hell'd he do this time?"

"Open container in a motor vehicle, possession of drug paraphernalia, no operator's license, expired tags, and failure to yield.

"Woooooo! He's looking at six months in County. Remember that time he got his ass beat out at the Eagles? Who did that again?"

"Matt Connor and Mikey Allen."

"That's right. I was in basic trainin'. I wish I'd seen it."

"They beat the dog shit outta him for sayin' Mikey's breath smelled like a rotten asshole."

Dickey laughed with his mouth wide open.

"Poor Lester was cryin' like a baby," Booty said.

"Cryin'? You mean like a bitch? With tears? Real cryin'? Or was he just whinin' and moanin'?"

"I'm talkin' tears, man. Red-faced. Sobbin' and blowin' snot bubbles."

"Are you serious?"

"I'm dead serious."

"Holy shit," Dickey replied, shaking his head. "I never woulda thunk that about old Lester. That's a shame."

Booty nodded, "I know, man. Cryin' like a little girl."

"Wow," Dickey said.

Booty folded the paper and laid it on the stacked milk crates they used as an end table. "I'm hungry as hell. Let's get a pizza."

"Aight. Furio's or Dominos?"

"Furio's," Booty answered. "Dominos gives me the runs."

Dickey drained his beer, belched loudly, then walked out to the front porch and picked up one of the dozen weekly advertisers scattered about on the steps. He walked back inside, removed the flier from its plastic bag, rifled through the pages until he found a Furio's Pizza coupon, and threw the rest on the floor.

"Git me a Dr Peppers," Booty said.

Dickey didn't respond as he dialed the number on the coupon.

"Furio's. Can you hold, please?"

"I reckon."

Dickey sucked his teeth and admired his forearms and knuckle tattoos while he waited.

"Sorry about your wait. How can I help you?"

"I'd like to order a pizza."

"Pick up or delivery?"

"Delivery."

"What's the address, please?"

"One one eight, Budd Street."

"One one eight what street?"

"Budd."

"Bug?"

"No. Budd!"

"Can you spell it?

"B as in Budd. U as in, uh, uh… Ugly motherfucker. D as innnnn… umm… Dog. D as in, uh, uhhhhh Damn dirty ass dog went and shit on the floor."

"Oh, Budd."

"That's right. Budd."

"What can I get you?"

"A large pepperoni and mushroom with a Dr Peppers and a Orange Crush."

"That's a large pepperoni and mushroom with one Dr Pepper and one Orange Crush?"

"That's right, killer. And throw in some crushed red pepper, parmesan cheese, salt, 'nana peppers, garlic butter, and a couple peppermints."

"Anything else?"

"And some plates and napkins."

"That'll be ten dollars and fifty-nine cents."

"I got a dollar-off coupon."

"That'll be nine dollars and fifty-three cents."

"Alrighty then."

"Give us about thirty minutes."

"Alright now."

"Thank you."

Dickey hung up the phone.

"We better get packed while we're waiting for the pizza," Booty said.

"How long you reckon we'll be gone?" Dickey asked.

Booty pulled a gray backpack from under his bed. "Down to Kentucky and back? We might be back tomorrow night. I'd plan for a day or maybe two, though. You know how these things go sometimes."

"We ain't never dealt directly with no cartel guys before. I'm not sure I like it."

'We ain't dealing with no cartel guys. We're just droppin' off and pickin' up. All the dealin's done happened. Everything's gonna be fine."

"Yeah. You're probably right."

Booty stuffed a tee shirt, a toothbrush, toothpaste, deodorant, and two packs of Chesterfields into his backpack. Then he took a Ruger .357 Magnum and a box of shells from the top drawer of his dresser and a hunting knife in a leather sheath from the shelf of his closet. "I'm all set," he said.

Dickey was rummaging around in an old footlocker he kept at the end of his bed. "I'm almost done."

Bootie held out his hand and said, "I'll wait for the pizza."

Dickey stared at Booty's hand. "You need something?"

"I need some cash if you wanna eat pizza."

Dickey sighed. "Here, Wilbur," he said while reaching into his pocket and handing Booty a wrinkled five-dollar bill."

"Don't call me Wilbur," Booty said and returned to the living room.

Dickey laid a large duffel bag and a backpack out on the bed, then walked to his dresser and closet and brought back two changes of clothes and an extra pair of underwear. Then he went to the bathroom and retrieved a toothbrush, toothpaste, deodorant, a bottle of Tylenol, a bottle of Motrin, a bottle of Vivarin, a box of Band-Aids, two rolls of toilet paper, and a bottle of hydrogen peroxide, all of which he laid on his bed. He took a light blanket from the footlocker, along with two cans of Sterno, a can opener, two plastic bowls, two aluminum coffee cups, two forks, two spoons, a medium-sized pan with a lid, a large pocketknife, and a hunting knife. Dickey then went into the kitchen and brought back a jar of Taster's Choice, a box of oatmeal cream pies, a dozen cans of Vienna sausages, a half dozen packs of Ramen noodles, a box of Ritz crackers, a bottle of hot sauce, a gallon jug full of water, and a pint of Wild Turkey. Finally, he pulled a Glock nine-millimeter pistol and a Ruger Mini 14 rifle, each with three fully loaded magazines and an extra box of shells, from under his bed. Everything was placed neatly into his bags, except for the pistol and the hunting knife, which he would carry on his person. Then he took the bags into the living room, set them by the front door, and said, "I'm ready to roll."

Booty looked up. "Holy shit, man. Are you sure you didn't forget nothin'?"

Dickey looked down at his bags lying on the floor, then returned to the bedroom. A few minutes later, he returned with a candle, an umbrella, and two folded ponchos in zip-lock bags.

Booty looked bewildered. "Are you serious right now?"

"What if it rains?"

Just then, there was a knock at the door. Dickey peeked through the peephole. "Pizza's here."

When Dickey opened the door, a skinny, nervous-looking young man with greasy hair and a pimply face stood before him, holding a pizza box with two bottles of pop on top. He said nothing, and Dickie stared at him for a few seconds. "Well," Dickie said. "You want somethin'?"

"I'm delivering your pizza," the young man responded.

"Okay."

The young man said nothing as Dickey took the pizza and bottles of pop from him, turned, and handed them to

Booty. Then he turned back to the pizza delivery guy. "Thanks, buddy. You have a good evenin' now." Then he shut the door.

"Ain't you gonna pay for the pizza?" Booty asked, still holding the money in his hand.

"I was, but he never asked me for it."

There was another knock at the door. Dickey opened it. It was the pizza delivery man again.

"The pizza is nine fifty-three," the young man said quietly, his eyes shifting left and right.

"Here you go," Dickey responded, handing over nine dollars and fifty-five cents. "Go ahead and keep the change."

The young man spun on his heels and hurried back to his car.

"Dig in, man," Dickey said.

Booty laughed. "Hand me my Dr Peppers."

PART THREE

The following day, Booty and Dickey had a cup of coffee and a cigarette for breakfast, loaded their bags into Booty's car, and headed to Greenfield Textiles to pick up the truck.

Pulling into the parking lot, Booty motioned toward the truck. "There's our ride." Then he pulled in next to it, switched off the ignition, and dropped the key on the floorboard.

They put their bags in the back seat and climbed in, with Booty in the driver's seat as usual. Dickey took the pistol from his waistband, climbed into the passenger seat, and opened the glove box. He took out the keys and handed them to Booty, then put his pistol inside the glove box and closed it.

"Let's get to work, Wilbur," Dickey said.

Booty started the truck, backed out, and started towards Save a Lot. "It's seven o'clock. Plenty of time. And don't call me Wilbur."

When they pulled into Sav-A-Lot, they parked next to the blue Mercedes in the center of the lot. A young black man was sitting behind the wheel. He was drinking coffee from a paper cup, bobbing his head, and singing to himself in the rear-view mirror. For two minutes, he did this, ignoring the two guys who parked right next to him in the nearly empty lot. Finally, the young man looked at his watch, got out of his car, and walked to the truck.

The man removed his sunglasses and climbed into the truck's back seat. "Good morning," he said.

"You must be Terrence," Booty said.

"That's the rumor, " Terrence replied, offering his hand to Booty.

Booty shook his hand and said, "I'm Booty, and this is Dickey."

"Booty and Dickey? Are you shitting me?" Terrence asked with a grin while looking back and forth at the two men he had just met.

There was an awkward silence, then Dickey extended his hand to Terrence. "It's nice to meet you."

"Uh, yes, it's nice to meet you as well," Terrence replied, shaking Dickey's hand. "Let's get down to business."

Terrence handed Booty a large zip lock bag. Inside

were three Tracphones.

"Burner phones. We supposed to use these?" Booty asked.

"Yes. In fact, go ahead and turn your personal phones off."

Booty and Dickey did as they were asked.

"The phones are numbered one through three. You're to use one phone daily to place calls to or receive calls from Tom Allen only. No calls are to be placed to any other number. If another number calls this phone, do not answer and destroy the phone immediately. Mr. Allen has three phones as well. His daily number is written on each phone in Sharpie. That's the only number you call, and that's the only number you answer calls from. Every night at one second past midnight, you destroy the phone from the day before and turn on the next one. Do you understand?

"We understand," Booty answered.

"The drive to Junction City is about three hours and forty minutes going the speed limit. You'll be on the road at eight-fifteen this morning. That'll put you there no later than one o'clock, with a couple of pit stops. Phil will meet you there."

"What route are we taking?" Booty asked.

"Good question." Terrence handed Booty two sheets of paper with a hand-drawn map and written directions. "You're taking the back way through Hillsboro, down US 62 to Ripley, Maysville, past Blue Licks Battlefield, Paris, and into Lexington. From there, it's an hour or so to Junction City out in the sticks.

Booty nodded his head.

Terrence reached into his back pocket and took out a ragged manila envelope. "I suspect you'll want this."

"Now we're getting somewhere," Dickey said with a

grin.

"There's fifteen hundred in there, along with a two-hundred-dollar prepaid Visa Card for expenses. When you get back, there'll be another envelope under the driver's seat of your car. It'll be parked at Sav a Lot. Park this truck next to your car, leave the keys and Visa card in the glove box, and be on your way. Your job will be done."

"Sounds simple enough," Booty said. Looking at Dickey.

"Easy peasy lemon squeezy," Dickey said in agreement.

"Great! You guys have a safe trip. I gotta get back to Columbus," Terrence said, putting his sunglasses on and opening the door to leave.

"Hang on," Booty said.

Terrence stopped in mid-motion.

"Where's the stuff we're delivering to Phil the Pill?"

Terrence smiled. "Damn near forgot about that. It's in the trunk of your car at the textile plant. Go pick it up and get on the road."

PART FOUR

They were halfway to Hillsboro when the burner phone labeled "#1" rang. Dickey answered, "Good morning, Cap'n."

"You're on the road, I assume?" Tom Allen asked.

"Yessir. Left Greenfield almost fifteen minutes ago."

"Good. Keep your speed down, and don't draw attention to yourselves. Check in when you get to Lexington."

"10-4, Cap'n"

"Knock that Cap'n shit off, asshole."

Dickey hung up the phone.

"What'd he say," Booty asked.

"Said to keep the speed down and don't draw any attention to ourself. Said to call him when we get to Lexington."

"Is that it?"

"Said to go ahead and get into Phil's package and roll us up a fat boy to smoke."

"Bullshit!"

"Maybe I misheard him."

"Why do you antagonize him, Dickey?"

Dickey thought for a minute. "Because I can, and I know he'll just put up with it. He has to understand that he can't always control everything around him."

When they got to Ripley, Booty pulled the truck into McDonald's to use the restroom and buy breakfast.

"We eatin' here or takin' it to go," Dickey asked as they walked in the door."

"Let's take it to go," Booty said. I wanna git down the road."

"Alrighty then."

Booty ordered while Dickey went to the restroom. Then Dickey waited on the food while Booty went.

When the order was ready, Dickey walked out the door, put the food and drinks in the truck, lit a cigarette, and stood on the curb to smoke it while he waited for Booty to come out. Across the lot was a white Honda Accord with two men inside, one of whom Dickey thought he recognized. The men were looking at Dickey, and when they saw him looking back at them, they drove away. Dickey thought things may have just gotten complicated and instinctively patted the handgun tucked in his waistband.

When Booty came out, Dickey didn't mention the car and the two guys inside. As they ate breakfast, Booty drove out of Ripley, passed through Aberdeen, and crossed the bridge over the Ohio River into Maysville, Kentucky.

"We just added ten years to our sentence if we get caught," Dickey said. "Crossing state lines is a big deal to the law."

"We ain't gettin' caught."

"These hash browns give me heartburn. Pull into KMart and let me get some Tums," Dickey said, pointing to the KMart on their right.

Booty pulled into the lot and dropped Dickey off at the door. Then he drove to the back of the parking lot, pulled in between an old red Camaro and a rusted-out Chevy truck, laid his seat back, turned the radio on, and dosed off to George Strait singing about Amarillo.

Dickey walked out of K-Mart and stood scanning the parking lot, looking for the truck. "Dammit, Booty," he muttered to himself. Dickey took the bottle of Tums out of the bag and stuck it in his jacket pocket. Then he threw the bag in the trash, lit a cigarette, and started walking through the parking lot looking for Booty. Walking past the cart return, he noticed a white Honda with the windows down and "I'll Whip Ya Head Boy" by 50 Cent blaring from the speakers. Well, shit, Dickey thought. Here we go.

"Dickey Dance! Da fuck, boy? Why you in Maysville, nigga?"

Dickey stopped in his tracks and started to reach for his pistol but knew that was a bad idea.

"You bein' sloppy, Dickey."

"Excuse me?" Dickey responded.

"You doin' sloppy work. Bein' reckless."

"I know you," Dickey said, pointing a finger at the passenger. You're Duck Wing or some shit like that. We've met before. The first time was in Fort Wayne two or three years ago. You and your homies was settin' up a Coppin Zone to sell Scooby Snacks to school kids. The second time was in Greenfield last April. I saw you at Rhoda Polly's house passed out over a footstool with "Git In Nigga" wrote on your ass in red lipstick. Some fat fucker wearing a gimp mask was preppin' your ass for the Dayton black snake. You wouldn't remember that one."

"It's Du-Quayne, mutha fucka. And you must be gettin' me confused with someone else."

"I don't think so," Dickey said, before turning to the driver, a big man weighing nearly three hundred pounds. "What's your name, sunshine?"

The man didn't respond. He just stared at Dickey through a pair of orange-framed sunglasses.

"He ain't have much to say," Du-Quayne said. He's more a man of action if you know what I'm sayin'."

"I saw you back in Ripley," Dickey said.

"See what I mean? We been tailin' you since you left your house this morning. But you ain't seen us until Ripley? That's sloppy. That dumb fuck brother of yours been drivin' fast, rollin' through stop signs. Beggin' to get pulled over."

"Why you followin' us?"

"Why you messin' around with the status quo? Two homeless-lookin' redneck cracker fucks, gonna go do business with the cartel?"

Dickey started to respond, but the driver stepped from the car and walked toward him. The man reminded Dickey of a black Boss Hogg but taller. He got up close to Dickey and growled like a dog.

Du-Quayne spoke again, "Look. Y'all tighten yo shit up. Stay focused. Keep movin', and don't draw attention to yourselves. We on your side. They might be people out here who ain't. You dig what I'm sayin'?"

Dickey turned to look at Du-Quayne and then back at the big man. "Yeah. I dig."

"You make sure this thing goes smooth like butter. We gonna be watchin'. When the deal's done, we all goin' back to Greenfield and sit down with Tom Allen to hammer out a new arrangement. Got it?"

Dickey didn't answer.

"Use your hillbilly head for somethin' more than a coon huntin' hat rack. Play it smart. You dig?"

"Are you fuckin' done?"

"Y'all muthafuckas smell like wet chickens," Du-Quanye answered, wrinkling his nose. "Come on, Marvin. I'm hungry as fuck."

The big man turned and got back into the car with Du-Quayne.

"I'll be seeing you soon, I hope. Nice to meet you, Marvin," Dickey said with a big smile.

The Honda pulled away, and Dickey continued his search for Booty.

Dickey finally found Booty snoozing like a passed-out wino at the back of the lot. Dickey tried to open the passenger side door, but it was locked. He considered busting out a window, but decided to tap on it instead. It took a full minute, but Booty finally awakened and unlocked the door.

"What took you so long?" Booty asked.

'What the hell were you doing out here?" Dickey responded.

"I was restin' my eyes."

Dickey got in the truck without responding, and they pulled out and got back on the road.

"We got trouble," Dickie said as they left Maysville and continued south on US 68. He commenced telling Booty about his run-in with the Detroit boys, how they had been following them since they left Greenfield, and that they wanted to go to Greenfield and work out a new deal with Tom Allen once the cartel's shipment was delivered.

Booty listened, then immediately called Tom Allen and told him about Dickey's encounter with the two men from Detroit.

"Flashy-lookin' guy. Dressed like he's dancin' on Soul Train. Dufraine or some shit like that."

"Du-Quayne Greene. He's Mack Daddy Greene's boy. Dangerous. He won't come at you face to face. Don't turn your back on him, though. He ain't afraid to leave a mark. He's a homo. Not that it means much. Fag or not, he's dangerous."

"What about the other guy?"

"I don't know him. Probably just some meathead. What's his name again?"

"Dickey said Du-Quayne called him Marvin."

"I don't know. I'll ask around."

"What do we do?"

"Dammit to hell," Tom said. "I had hoped Detroit would just let it pass. It's one damn shipment."

"You think these guys will try anything?" Booty asked.

"These two are just keeping an eye on things. I suspect there are more, though, and they might try a smash-and-grab once the transfer is made and you're headed home."

"I don't like the sound of that. Do we call it off?"

"Let me think about this. Call me when you get to Lexington," Tom said, hanging up the phone.

When Booty saw the entrance to Blue Lick's Battlefield, he pulled in and parked near the museum.

"Now what, Wilbur?" Dickey asked. "I'd say we have a crisis on our hands."

"I don't know, Dickey. I just don't know. Stop callin' me fuckin' Wilbur."

Just then, a white Honda Accord pulled up beside them, with Du-Quayne hanging out the window.

"Yo! Booty and Dickey! I didn't know y'all was here. Did you know this is where Daniel Boone's boy was killed? Ain't that some shit? Israel Boone. That's a badass name. I like that!"

Dickey rolled his window down.

"You're like a bad smell. Do you know that? You're hard to git rid of."

Du-Quayne looked over the top of his glasses. "What? You don't wanna hang out, Dickey? That hurts my feelings."

"Hurt feeling's ain't all you're gonna have if you keep gettin' in the way, Duck Wing."

Du-Quayne pointed a finger pistol at Dickey and mouthed, "Bang."

"I'll be waitin'," Dickey said, looking straight at Du-Quayne.

"Let's git Marvin," Du-Quayne said.

Marvin punched the accelerator to the floor, and the Honda fishtailed out of the parking lot and back onto US 62, heading south.

When they got to Millersburg, Dickey noticed Du-Quayne and Marvin standing near an Amish food stand that sold fried pies and coffee. Du-Quayne was holding a cup of coffee and Marvin had a mouthful of pie and another pie in his right hand. As Booty pulled the truck up to a stoplight, Du-Quayne saw them.

"Yo! Booty and Dickhead! Ya'll gotta try these pies. They good as hell, boy!"

Then as if on cue, Du-Quayne, Marvin, and a skinny Amish kid about fourteen years old gave Booty and Dickey the finger just as the light turned green.

"I hate those assholes," Dickey announced.

They drove along in silence for twenty miles, when Dickey, who had taken about all he could take, said, "Pull over at this Shell station."

"What for?" Booty asked.

"I'm gonna have a talk with our shadows."

Dickey was not the brains behind his and Booty's limited success. Dickey was aware of that and didn't care. In fact, he was happy not to be in charge. He didn't have to make plans or think of solutions to things that could happen but probably wouldn't. Looking ahead was not what Dickey was good at. He was good, very good, at making split-second decisions and taking decisive action on the fly. Booty understood that, and he had learned to rely on it during uncertain situations.

Booty whipped the car into the Shell Station.

"Park up by the front door," Dickey said.

Booty did as instructed, and Dickey exited the vehicle and went inside.

Du-Quayne and Marvin pulled in thirty seconds later and parked next to Booty. "Why'd you stop?" Du-Quayne asked.

"Dickey had to pee," Booty answered.

Five minutes went by. "What's taking him so long?"

"I don't know. Maybe he had to poop too."

Du-Quayne looked at Marvin. "Go see what's takin' that prick so long."

Marvin exited the vehicle and walked inside the store. He scanned the area looking for Dickey and didn't see him, so he walked to the back and turned the knob on the men's room door. It was locked, so Marvin knocked on the door. "You die in there or somethin', Dickey?"

There was no answer.

"Get moving muthafucka. We gotta go."

The toilet flushed, and water ran in the sink before a thin elderly man shuffled out and looked at Marvin. "It's all yours, buddy. Better light a match."

"What da fuck?" Marvin looked around and focused on the door with the "Employees Only" sign, opened it, and walked through.

Where'd that asshole go? Marvin strolled past a dirty mop sink and a rack of mops and brooms, eyes darting left and right, looking for Dickey. Past boxes of potato chips, candy bars on pallets, and cases of pop stacked to the ceiling.

Suddenly, someone grabbed Marvin from behind and held a knife to his throat. "You lookin' for me, fat boy?"

"Dickey! Come on now, man. Don't do nothin' stupid."

"Shut up."

Dickey reached under Marvin's jacket and removed the pistol inside. Then, in one motion, he pulled the knife from Marvin's throat and put the pistol against his back while shoving him towards the back door.

"Go on outside. Real slow," Dickey said.

Marvin did as he was told.

"Now what? You gonna kill me? Marvin asked, his voice trembling.

"With God as my witness, Marvin, I don't wanna hurt

you. But I will if you don't leave me any other choice. That makes sense, right?"

"Yeah. Yeah. It makes sense."

"Bottom line is, I'm tired of seeing you and your boyfriend's face every time I look up. I'm tired of the threats and the smart talk. Me and Booty is gonna do our job. No matter if you're around or not. We ain't doin' nothin' different by you bein' up our asses. This whole cartel, Detroit, distribution, blah, blah, blah shit is above our pay grade anyway. Am I right? Let the big shots work it out. Does that make sense, Marvin?

"Yeah. I'm gettin' what you're sayin'.

Good! So, you got three choices. And the first choice is probably your best one. Keep trailing us, but leave us the fuck alone. Enjoy the scenic drive. Stop down the road in Paris. There's a Popeyes there. Have a four-piece box and a sweet tea. Spend a couple hours driving around and looking at the horse farms. They're really nice! Just let us do our jobs, and we'll all be happy in the end. The second choice is to turn around and go back where you come from right now. That's probably not a good choice though, 'cause your boss wouldn't like that. Would he?"

"Nah, man."

Dickey's face suddenly took on a dead serious expression. He moved in closer and spoke quietly and directly into Marvin's ear.. "I hope you're hearin' what I'm sayin', Marvin."

Marvin swallowed hard. "Yeah. I'm with ya."

"Good. Cause your third choice is to keep fuckin' around with me and Booty. And you know what, Marvin? That's the worst choice of all. Cause if you do that. Listen to me, Marvin. Listen closely. If you do that, I'm gonna go all Greenfield on your ass. And that'll suck. For you, I mean. Not for me." Dickey let his words sink in. "I gotta know we're cool. Are we cool, Marvin?"

"Oh, yeah. Yeah, we cool."

Dickey smiled. "That's good. That's real good, Marvin. You and me is finally on the same page. We're cool. I mean, I feel like we're cool. Are we really cool?" Dickey pressed the pistol hard into Marvin's back.

"Yeah, man. We cool."

"Good! Be sure to explain that to Du-Quayne. Tell him that me and you have reasoned together; figured it all out, and we're cool. Make sure he's cool, too, Marvin. That way, we can all go home in one piece and let the big shots figure all this bullshit out."

Marvin shook his quickly head up and down.

Otherwise, what happens, Marvin?

Marvin looked back at Dickey with a blank look on his face.

"What's gonna happen if we all ain't cool, Marvin?"

Marvin cleared his throat. "You gonna go all Greenfield on someone's ass."

"Not someone's ass. Nooooooooo. No sir! Whose ass am I gonna go all Greenfield on?"

"Mine."

"And who else's?"

"Du-Quayne's."

"That's right! You got it! I am gonna go Greenfield on Marvin's and Du-Quayne's asses."

Dickey lowered the gun, dropped the magazine into his hand, racked the slide to clear the chamber, and kicked the ejected round into a sewer grate. "Let's get back on the road."

"Du-Quayne gonna ask where we been. What do I say?"

Dickey used his thumb to push the rounds out of Marvin's magazine and into his front pocket. "Tell 'em we been reasoning together."

Marvin nodded. "Reasoning together."

Dickey handed Marvin his empty pistol and magazine, then motioned for him to walk in front as they cut back through the store and to their vehicles parked out front.

Du-Quayne looked up as Dickey and Marvin came out the door. "Holy shit! My ass is falling asleep sittin' here." Du-Quayne pointed at Booty. "That muthafucka dry as hell, boy. How you ride with him all the way down here, Dickey? I was tryin' to be sociable. He act like he ain't hear a word I say."

"Maybe you just ain't that interesting," Dickey said.

"Shit. He prolly a racist. The hell you two doin' in there anyway? Havin' a booty call? Get it?" Du-Quayne laughed hysterically while pointing at Booty.

Dickey smiled. "I'm sure Marvin will fill ya in. Now, we got an appointment we gotta get to. You ladies have a good day. And lay back a little. You might start drawing attention."

Du-Quayne wrinkled his forehead. "You be careful, Dickey. I'll be close by if you need me." Then he nodded at Marvin, who backed the car out and sped south on 68 towards Paris.

"What the fuck just happened, Dickey?" Booty said, obviously annoyed.

"I explained to Marvin that them bein' up our asses ain't gonna make no difference in me and you doin' what we're paid to do. I also explained what's gonna happen if they decide to keep being up our asses. I think he understands." Dickey's eyes narrowed as he turned to look at Booty. "I don't think Du-Quayne will understand, though."

"We need a plan, Dickey. And we ain't got a lot of time to make one."

149

"Makin' plans is your job. I'm gonna catch a nap. Wake me up when we get to Lexington."

Just as they entered Paris, the burner phone rang, and Booty pulled the truck into the parking lot of an adult bookstore called The Gilded Rhino. Dickey woke up with a start and grabbed at the steering wheel.

"Chill out, man! Tom's callin'! I pulled over to answer the phone," Booty said, pushing Dickey back into his seat.

"Holy shit, man. I thought we was gettin' lit up," Dickey said. His eyes were wide open and sweat ran down his face."

"It's all good man. It's all good. Just relax." Booty patted Dickey's leg. "We're okay."

"I just need a minute."

"I'm gonna call Tom back. Why don't you roll the window down and get some air."

"Where are we at anyway? Lexington?"

"No. Paris."

Dickey looked out the window. "The Gilded Rhino. Adult movies, magazines, and novelties. Hell, I'm gonna go in and get me a fuck book. You want anything? Butt plug, nipple clamps, lube?"

"I'm good. Thanks, though."

Dickey laughed, got out of the car, and walked inside.

Tom answered the phone on the first ring.

"Sorry, boss," Booty said. "We was in the Burger King drive-thru when you called."

There's a change in plans. Everything is getting moved back a day. They couldn't get off the ground in Aguascalientes. Too many Federales snooping around. They're going to try again first thing tomorrow morning. I want you to drive down to Danville and spend the night. Get a room at the Travelodge. There's a Mexican restaurant across the street called La Cristina's. Go in and ask for

Miguel. He's expecting you. He'll feed you and take care of your room."

"That sounds like some shit out of a movie, Boss."

"The cartel's roots run deep. Miguel will let you know when to head to Junction City tomorrow. It's just ten or twelve minutes down the road."

"Okay."

"Don't be out running around. Keep a low profile."

"Will do, boss."

"Any questions?"

"What are we going to do about these two Detroit guys that's followin' us? Dickey tried to make them understand that we ain't playing their games. I'm not sure they get it, though. I feel like they are gonna hit us somewhere along the road on our way back to Greenfield."

"I'm sending a couple guys down to meet you on the way back. They'll be your wingmen and escort you home. I'll arrange for them to meet you in Lexington."

"What if we don't make it to Lexington?"

"If they hit you, it'll be between Lexington and Hillsboro. Some desolate stretch of road. If they try anything before you get to Lexington, do whatever you have to do to get away."

"Do anything? Are you sure about that?"

"I want that shipment brought back to Greenfield. You understand me? You do whatever it takes to make that happen. Are we clear?"

"Clear as clean glass, boss."

"Good."

Tom hung up, and Booty felt a sense of dread coming over him. Just then, Dickey came bounding out the door of the Gilded Rhino and got back in the car.

"Hey, man. What did Tom Allen say?" Dickey asked.

"I'll fill you in on the way to Danville."

151

"Danville?"

"Yeah. There's been a change in plans."

"Well, I got two fuck books, "Butts and Boobs" and "Asian Dream Girls." Start talking while I start reading."

PART FIVE

Booty and Dickey pulled into the Danville Travelodge at three fifty-nine p.m. and parked near the back of the lot. "There's the Mexican restaurant," Booty said, pointing across the parking lot. "I'm gonna go talk to this Miguel fella about gettin' us a room."

Dickey nodded, and Booty walked to La Cristina's Mexican Restaurant across the road. It was nearly empty when he stepped inside. A young man with a menu in his hand approached Booty and said, "Good afternoon, Senor. How many?"

"I'm lookin' for Miguel," Booty replied. "Are you Miguel?"

The young man pointed across the restaurant to a short, pudgy, middle-aged man wiping a tabletop with a rag. "That's Miguel."

Booty walked across the restaurant and said to the man wiping off the table, "Miguel, I'm Booty. Tom Allen sent me."

Miguel didn't look up. "Hello, Senor. Your room number is 326. Go to the front desk and tell them you are

Mr. White. They will give you your key."

"What about supper?"

Miguel finished with the table and turned to face Booty. "I will bring it to you at seven o'clock. Do you like chicken or beef?"

"Uhhh. Chicken, I guess."

"And your partner?"

"Beef."

"I will see you at seven o'clock. Now, I have to finish cleaning up. We will be busy soon."

"Okay. Thank you."

Miguel smiled and walked away.

As Booty returned to the motel parking lot, he couldn't help but think how uncartel-like Miguel looked.

The desk clerk, a gay man in his late thirties named Casey, looked Booty and Dickey up and down when they walked through the door. He seemed especially taken with Dickey and directed his attention to him, although Booty did all the talking. After telling them about the pool and fitness center (which consisted of an old stationary bike, an ancient treadmill, and a couple sets of dumbbells), he mentioned that a continental breakfast was served in the lobby between six and nine am, then reminded them that if they needed ANYTHING. They, or more precisely Dickey, should call the front desk as he would be on duty until one a.m.

At precisely seven o'clock, there was a knock on the door. Booty and Dickey picked up their handguns lying on the table, then Booty went to the door and looked through the peephole. It was Miguel.

Miguel brought two bags full of food, including chicken fajitas, a steak quesadilla, a half dozen tacos, a bag of tortilla chips, and several small plastic containers of salsa, as well as two Jaritos sodas and two ice-cold bottles of Corona with slices of lime.

"Thank you, Miguel," Booty said.

"Gracias," Dickey added.

Miguel simply nodded. "You must be there tomorrow morning at eight o'clock. Do not be late. I hope you know where to go because no one has told me. Your contact will be waiting for you".

"Eight o'clock. Got it," Booty answered.

"There were two men, two black men, looking for you at the restaurant."

"What did you tell them?" Dickey asked.

"I told them I didn't speak English. I saw them parked in the motel parking lot when I arrived."

"Thanks for the heads up," Booty said.

Booty opened the door for Miguel, who stopped halfway out and said, "I will be in the restaurant until midnight if you need anything. I wish you good luck. May God protect you."

When Miguel was gone, Booty and Dickey went to the window and looked out at their truck in the lot below. The white Honda Accord with Du-Quayne and Marvin inside was parked next to their vehicle, with the windows down and a cloud of smoke pouring into the air.

"Well, I hope they get a great night's sleep. Poor dears," Dickey said.

"Screw 'em. Let's eat before the food gets cold," Booty said while tearing into the bags.

"This reminds me of when I was in Iraq," Dickey said. "We was living in one of Sadamn's palaces in Baghdad. There was about twenty-five of us. We was detached from our battalion and sent out to this little island in the Tigris to secure a dozen sheds that the CIA thought might have weapons in 'em. When we got out there, we didn't find any weapons, but we did find big bales of marijuana and hashish, along with hundreds of cases of American whiskey. Our Lieutenant, a big country boy from Fairhope, Alabama named Bob Lee, told us to load as much of that shit as we could on our rubber boats and get it back to the palace that night after it got dark. We musta took two hundred pounds of weed and hash along with twenty cases of whiskey. There was still ten times that much in the shacks, so Lieutenant Lee reported it back to the CIA, and they sent out some of their guys the next day to burn it down. I guess our battalion forgot about us because we stayed in that palace for over two weeks eatin' Sadamn's food, smokin' his weed, and drinkin' his whiskey. It was like a scene outta *Apocalypse Now*. Finally, we got called back to our battalion and headed north to kill insurgents. We sold the leftover drugs and whiskey to some Marines who had occupied the little airport next to the palace."

"That's some crazy shit, man," Booty replied while stuffing his mouth with chicken fajitas. Tell me again how many ragheads you killed over there."

"Five for sure. Probably closer to a dozen, though."

"Does it ever bug you? I mean killin' them people."

"Why would it? Those goat fuckers were tryin' to kill me, weren't they?

"Did you like it?"

"Like what? Killin' Hajis? Hand that bag of tacos over here."

Booty passed the bag of tacos. "Yeah, did you wanna git em?"

"At first, it wasn't so much that I wanted to git em. It was more like they needed got. After a couple months, though, I kinda liked it. It's an acquired taste, I guess."

"I'd gone with you, Dickey. I mean, if I wasn't in prison at the time."

"I know you woulda. I'd prolly went to prison with you if I wasn't in the Army at the time."

They both laughed, then Dickey belched loudly and lit a cigarette.

"You know it's a nonsmoking room, don't you?" Booty asked.

"I saw the sign, Wilbur," Dickey answered as he held the pack of cigarettes out to Booty."

Booty took a cigarette and said, "You can't follow the simplest rules, can you?"

"That's why I ain't in the Army no more."

Booty lit his cigarette, exhaled a plume of smoke, and said, "Don't call me Wilbur."

"What the hell we gonna do with the money we make off this clusterfuck anyway?" Dickey asked

Booty started to speak, then stopped.

"You got your wheels a spinnin'," Dickey said, wagging his finger at Booty.

"I wanna go to Florida."

"Man, you been talkin' bout that ever since the parents went down there ten years ago. Why ain't you already went?"

"I don't know. Money, I reckon. Lots of reasons. Maybe I don't really wanna leave."

"You said you wanted the hell outta Greenfield a thousand times."

"Everyone I know says they want outta Greenfield. How many ever leave, though?"

"You should go."

"You want me to go?"

"Hell no. But you need to go. You ain't doin' nothing in Greenfield cept things you shouldn't be doin' and tryin' not to git caught. It's been that way your whole life. Mine too."

"You think I'll be different in Florida?"

"Maybe."

"I'll think about it."

"Wilbur, how…"

"Don't call me Wilbur."

"How much money you reckon is in that canvas bag Tom Allen gave us for the Mexicans? I figure there must be at least a hundred grand. Maybe more."

"I'd say that's about right. Why?"

"Just wonderin'. That's a lot of money."

Booty checked the clock on the nightstand. It said 12:08 a.m." It's time to change phones," he said to Dickey.

"I got it," Dickey said before picking the phone up and removing the battery. Then he walked into the bathroom, ran water in the sink, and dropped in the phone. "That oughta do it."

"We better hit the sack," Booty said. "No tellin' how tomorrow's gonna turn out."

"Roger that," Dickey answered. "I call the side closest to the bathroom."

Booty turned on phone number two, then walked to the window and looked over the parking lot. Miguel pushed a cart filled with trash bags to the dumpster at La Cristina's, red and blue lights flashed through the night sky from a traffic stop on the road, and smoke still rolled out of the windows of the Honda Accord.

"You know, Dickey…" Booty turned around to finish his sentence, but didn't. Dickey was already snoring.

PART SIX

Dickey woke up at five thirty the following morning, got out of bed, showered, and went downstairs for coffee. When he returned to the room, Booty was putting on his shoes.

"Booty," Dickey said.

"What?" Booty answered without looking up.

"You know why I ain't ever lost a fight?"

"Cause you fight pussies?"

"Cause I ain't afraid to strike first. You gotta be willin' to strike when the time comes without fear of what might happen next. There are times when you have to consider the consequences of your actions. There are other times you just have to strike."

Booty looked at Dickey but didn't respond."

"Remember I said that, brother."

"What's the matter, Dickey?"

"I got an uneasy feelin'. I've had the same feelin' twice in my life. Both times in Iraq. Both times, I lost people. Good people. I don't want to lose no more good people."

"Everything's gonna be fine. You'll see."

"I hope you're right, Booty. But if things start to go south, I ain't gonna hesitate to strike. And you can't hesitate either."

"I won't hesitate to strike."

Booty and Dickey looked at each other without speaking.

Booty smiled. "You want a hug or something?"

Dickey put his hands up. "Don't even think about it, Wilbur."

"Always with the Wilbur shit," Booty said, smiling.

Dickey laughed. "Let's get some breakfast before it's

all gone."

"Continental," Booty said as they went out the door."

When they returned from breakfast, Booty and Dickey checked out of the hotel and walked to their truck. Still parked next to them was the white Honda Accord. The windows were down, and Du-Quayne and Marvin were fast asleep in the front seats. An empty Jim Beam bottle was on the ground by the driver's side door, and cocaine residue covered the dash.

Booty and Dickey looked at the two men passed out in the car.

"What do we do with these motherfuckers?" Dickey asked.

"Let 'em sleep, I guess."

"We can do that. Let's make 'em a little less comfortable, though."

Dickey sat his duffle bag on the ground and rummaged through it until he found a roll of silver duct tape.

"Help me out, Booty," Dickey said. "Hold Du-Quayne's hands together."

Booty did as Dickey asked and held Du-Quayne's hands together as Booty wrapped duct tape around his wrists and then around his hands and fingers, encasing them in one giant ball of duct tape the size of a volleyball. Du-Quayne didn't stir. Next, Dickey wrapped tape several times around Du-Quayne's forehead and the headrest, then around his face and neck, leaving his nose and mouth uncovered so he could breathe. Still, Du-Quayne didn't wake up.

"Marvin's turn," Dickey said.

Booty held Marvin's hands while Dickey taped them up like Du-Quayne's. When the roll of silver duct tape ran out, Dickey produced a roll of orange duct tape from his bag and proceeded to tape Marvin's head to the headrest. Like Du-Quayne, Marvin never stirred.

Booty and Dickey stood and admired their work for a moment. Then Dickey buckled both men into their seats with their seatbelts. Booty noticed car keys in the cup holder, so he picked them up, threw them across the parking lot, and watched them slide under a nearby minivan.

"There ya go. That oughta keep them rascals outta mischief for awhile."

Booty and Dickey laughed until they cried.

The burner phone in Booty's back pocket began to ring, and Booty answered it. "Good mornin', Tom."

"Mornin', Booty. You and Dickless ready to roll?"

Dickey heard the insult and mouthed "fuck you" at the phone in Booty's hand.

"Yessir. We're checked outta the hotel and gettin' in the truck now."

"Good. Drive to Junction City. There's a Hardee's at the intersection. Phil's inside. Pull into the lot and wait. Phil will come out and get into a green Silverado. Follow him to the airport."

"Hardee's. Green Silverado. Airport. Got it."

"Are those two assholes from Detroit still messin' around?"

"They're around, but they're tied up at the moment."

"Good. Call me when it's wrapped up. We'll talk about gettin' you safely back to Greenfield."

"Yes, sir. I'll call just as soon as we're done."

"One other thing. Let Phil talk to the Mexicans and try to handle everything through him."

"Will do, sir. Anything else?"

"That's it. Get it done."

The line went dead.

Booty and Dickey took one last look at the passed-out Du-Quayne and Marvin. Then they got In the truck and headed to Junction City.

PART SEVEN

Booty pulled the truck into the Hardee's lot and parked near the front door. Within a minute, a skinny man with long hair in a ponytail, wearing blue jeans and an Ohio State Buckeyes sweatshirt, walked out the door and past their truck without looking at them.

"Shit, that's Phil," Booty said, pointing at the man walking past. "He's skinny as a fence post. Last time I saw him, he was a Milk Dud shy of three hundred pounds."

"Maybe he has the AIDS," Dickey offered.

"That's him for sure. He might have lost weight, but he didn't lose that bigass hook nose."

"He's gettin' in the green Silverado. That's him, alright.

Booty and Dickey followed Phil out of the parking lot and onto the highway, keeping a distance between them of about five car lengths.

"You packin' your Smith and Wesson? Dickey asked.

"Yep. Got her in my waistband. The skinnin' knife is on my belt," Booty answered.

"Good. Put a handful of shells in your front pocket. I've got the nine in my waistband, an extra magazine in my back pocket, and knife on my belt. I also got the Mini 14 locked and loaded."

"I think we're ready," Booty said with a smile.

"Keep on your toes, Booty. Don't turn your back on any of these sons-a-bitches. Not Phil. Not none of 'em. You can't trust 'em. Not one bit."

"It's gonna be fine, Dickey."

"I'm not so sure. I hope you're right. But I just ain't sure. I got that feelin'. If things start to fall apart, I'm gonna go on offense. I ain't waitin' around and puttin' us in no position that's hard to git out of."

"Now, don't be goin' all John Wayne for no reason."

"I hope I don't have a reason, but if I do, I ain't waitin' around, and neither are you. We need to act. Don't hesitate."

"Airport Road. We must be gittin' close," Booty said as he made a right turn onto a country road.

Within seconds, they were pulled up to a chain link gate across the driveway that, according to the sign, belonged to the Boyle County Airport.

A round man wearing a security guard uniform opened the gate, then walked to the driver's side door of the green Silverado and started talking to Phil. Phil handed the guard a rolled-up manilla envelope that he tucked into his jacket pocket. Then he walked back inside the gate. A few seconds later, the guard returned through the gate in a Ford Escort hatchback with three other people inside and drove down the road and out of sight.

Phil proceeded to drive through the gate and into the airport. Booty and Dickey followed, then stopped again as Phil returned to close the gate.

The convoy of two trucks drove a short distance to a building known as "Hangar B," according to the sign.

After parking, Phil exited his truck and walked back to Booty and Dickey's truck. Booty lowered his window.

Phil the Pill was grinning a big toothy grin that looked

vaguely like Gomer Pyle.

"I can't believe this shit! Booty Wilson and Dickey Dance. Two of Greenfield's finest! How the hell you doin'?"

"Hey, Phil! It's good to see ya! How long's it been?"

"I was in lockup for three years and fourteen days. So, I guess it's been four years or so. Get out and let me see you, man!"

Booty got out of the truck, and so did Dickey.

"You look good, Booty," Phil said, shaking Booty's hand. "Maybe a little thin on top, but you ain't hardly changed." Phil glanced at Dickey. "Dickey, you ain't changed much either. How you doin'?"

"I hardly recognized you comin' out the door at Hardee's," Booty said.

"Me either," Dickey added. "If it weren't for that big fuckin' snout, I'd a thought you was just another tweaker."

"Fuckin' Dickey. You ain't changed none, huh?"

"Old dogs don't change their spots," Dickey retorted.

Phil shook his head. "Well said, Dickey. Very well said."

"Phil," Booty said. "How much weight you lost?"

"One hundred fifty-four pounds. I weighed three o eight when I went to prison. Lost half my body weight. Eatin' right and exercisin'. That's it. I'm gonna git some of this loose skin trimmed off when I start making a little cash."

Phil raised his shirt to reveal folds of loose skin hanging around his waist.

"That's fuckin' gross," Dickey said.

"So, you saved some cartel guy's life, huh?" Booty asked.

"Haha! Yes, I did. Fucker went face-first in the yard

and started sucking dirt. I saw him go down and ran to him. It reminded me of when my dad died. He face-planted the same way while mowing the lawn. Anyway, I ran over and did CPR on him until the EMTs came out. I thought he was dead, but he pulled through. His uncle decided to repay me. So here we are. I guess we're all gonna make out okay, huh?"

"I sure hope so," Booty replied.

"Let's git this shit on the road. You two love birds can rekindle the flame later," Dickey said.

"Come on inside," Phil said, pointing to the door of Hangar B.

The hangar didn't have any planes inside. It was more of a storage space. Shelves with spare parts and other supplies. Worktables, tools, wooden pallets of this and that. In the center of the room was a medium-sized card table and four folding chairs.

"Let's see the money," Phil said.

Booty dropped the canvas money bag on the table along with the key. "Here's your welcome home gift from your uncle too." Booty sat the suitcase on the table beside the moneybag.

"Yeah, buddy! That's what I'm talkin' about!"

Phil opened the money bag and took a look inside. Then he locked it and sat it back on the table.

"Ain't you afraid of somebody walkin' in here and wondering what the hell is goin' on?" Dickey asked, looking around suspiciously.

"Nah. It's all good. The car that pulled out when we were pullin' in, that was the security guard, air traffic controller, mechanic, and janitor. They are off on a well-paid extended breakfast break. Nobody here but us bad guys, Dickaroni."

"Good. Let's git movin'," Dickey said, still looking

aground uncomfortably. "I'm ready to git back to Greenfield."

Phil nodded. "Hold tight, and I'll bring 'em in."

Phil picked up the suitcase and walked out the door. Booty and Dickey watched through the window as he put the suitcase in his truck and walked back on board the plane.

"You need to stay calm," Booty said to Dickey.

"I just want to git this over with and get outta here. I don't like it."

"I'm right there with ya."

"You be ready to move if things go south."

Booty nodded. "Here they come."

Phil and a short, fat Mexican man dressed in a Hawaiian shirt, Bermuda shorts, and flip-flops walked off the plane and towards the hangar.

"Fucker just stepped off the Love Boat," Dickey said.

Phil and the Mexican man entered the hangar.

"Boys," Phil said, walking towards the table. "This is Caesar Perez. Senor Perez, this is Wilbur and Richard. They are representin' my uncle's interests."

Booty extended his hand, but Caesar ignored it.

Caesar turned to Phil. "I expected Tom Allen."

"Uh, yes. My uncle, Mr. Allen, is very busy with some urgent business at home and couldn't come today. He sends his apologies and regards."

"He has business more important than receiving a gift from Ramon Luis Dominguez?"

"I assure you that Mr. Allen means no disrespect, and he is uh… he is grateful for your generosity and understandin'," Phil said nervously.

"Can we get down to business?" Dickey asked.

Booty picked up the money bag. "We have the payment. If you're ready, we can go ahead and make the swap."

Caesar eyed the money bag, then took it from Booty and weighed it in his hand. "It feels a little light, ese. Are you trying to take advantage of me, maybe?"

Booty cleared his throat. "I can assure you that all the money is there, sir. I mean, senor."

"How much is here?"

"Well, I don't know for sure. Nobody ever told me that. It's however much your deal called for. Me and Dickey are just here to pay you and bring the shit…, I mean the shipment back to Greenfield."

Caesar again turned to Phil. "See the problem? I am talking to two mules. These pendejos don't know what the hell is going on. I should get back on the plane and return to Aguascalientes."

"Senor Perez, I promise…"

"Why don't you cut the bullshit macho man act and bring the goddamn dope in here?" Dickey interrupted. "We ain't got no time for your games."

"Dickey," Booty said almost desperately. "Remember what Tom said. No drama. Let's just do our job and git outta here, okay?"

Caesar fixed his gaze on Dickey. "I think you don't know who you're talking to."

"And I think you're about to learn that a big mouth and a fat ass ain't no superpower."

"Holy shit," Phil said, trying to defuse things. "Can you all finish measuring your dicks later? We got work to do."

Caesar looked at Dickey and smiled. "Phil is right. I don't want to hurt you, gringo. It would be too simple and I'd take no pleasure in it. Let's conduct our business and be done."

Dickey stared hard into Caesar's eyes but did not

respond.

"That's a great idea," Phil said. "I'm going to the plane and bringing Paco in with the stuff. Don't kill each other while I'm gone."

As Phil walked out, Caesar leaned in close to Dickey and whispered, "I'm not a very patient man. It's always been my shortcoming. Don't test me."

Dickey nodded and whispered back, "I also have a shortcoming and it's gotten me in trouble more times than I can count."

Caesar smiled. "And what is that, senor?"

"I talk without a filter. And I gotta say, you smell like a giant pile of donkey shit that's been washed in Old Spice."

Caesar didn't hesitate. He clawed at Dickey and attempted to take him to the ground, but Dickey pivoted to the left and caught the big man with a punch to the throat that dropped him to his knees. Then, quick as a cat, Dickey pulled the knife from the scabbard on his belt and drove it deep into Caesar's chest just below the sternum. Caesar's eyes widened, and he mouthed "bendita madre," then collapsed face-first onto the cement floor.

Booty couldn't believe his eyes. "Holy shit, man, you killed him! You fuckin' killed him. What the fuck, Dickey? What the fuck?"

Dickey wiped the knife blade on Caesar's shirt and put it back in its scabbard. "Brother, he's dead as a zombie's ghost. He put his hands on me though."

Booty looked out the window and saw Phil walk off the plane and back towards the hangar. "Shit! Here comes Phil."

Dickey pulled Caesar's body behind a pallet stacked high with boxes and covered it with a tarp that was laying on a table. There were five or six spots of blood, each the size of a quarter, on the floor. Dickey smeared it with his foot and rubbed it into the concrete as much as possible.

"What the hell are we gonna do? What are we gonna say to Phil?" Booty asked emphatically.

"It's all changed, man. We need a new plan, and this is the best I got. We're going to Florida."

"What?"

"That's the plan unless you got a better one. And here comes Phil, so you got about ten seconds to come up with one if you don't."

"Fuck me to tears!"

"There's three thousand dollars that Tom paid us. There's at least a hundred thousand in the canvas bag that he gave us for the Mexicans. The stuff we brought for Phil is worth around twenty thousand, and there ain't no telling how much the stuff the Mexicans have is worth. Quarter of a million, maybe? It's all ours, brother."

"You're outta your ever-lovin' mind, Dickey!"

"Maybe. But I done took the first step, Wilbur, and there ain't no steppin' back now. It's too late for that. We just need to keep going forward."

Sweat poured off Booty's face, and he glanced around the hangar like a man just wanting to run. "Damn you, Dickey," Booty said as he drew the .357 magnum from his waistband. "You've done it this time. And don't call me fuckin' Wilbur!"

Dickey looked out the window at the plane. "Here comes Phil. I'm bettin' one or two Mexicans come off that plane right behind him. That leaves the pilot on the plane. You deal with Phil and his pals when they come in. I'll cover you from the back."

"What?"

"Remember what I told you yesterday? You gotta be

willin' to act when the time comes. Without fear of what happens next."

"What? Yes, I remember."

"Now's the time."

"I went to school with Phil," Booty said. "I can't kill him. I've knowd him my whole life."

Dickey grabbed Booty by the arm.

"Dammit, Booty! You're thinking too damn much. Don't kill Phil. Kill the fuckin' drug lords. We'll deal with Phil later."

"Oh, yeah," Booty answered, his voice trembling.

"You got your whole life ahead of you. Don't waste your chance to make it better."

"I ain't never killed no one, Dickey. This shit ain't natural to me. I'm a thinker, not a fighter."

"Here he comes. You know what to do."

Dickey dove behind a row of toolboxes just as Phil came through the door.

Phil smiled broadly as he came through the door and walked towards Booty.

"Booty," Phil said. "There's enough dope on there to keep every tweaker in southern Ohio happy for the next ten years."

"Uh… That's good, Phil."

"They're bringin' it in. Where's the cash?"

Booty pointed to the canvas bag lying on the table.

"Where's Caesar?" Phil asked.

"Uh, he had to step out."

"Step out? To where?"

Just then, two Mexicans walked through the door and into the hangar.

One, a tall, thin man with a Fu Man Chu mustache and carrying an M4 rifle, positioned himself midway between the door and the table, while the other man, short and stocky, walked towards Booty with two large suitcases in tow."

"Buen dia, señor. I am Paco Duran," the man said, extending his hand.

Booty's eyes darted left and right before shaking Paco's hand.

"Mornin'. I'm Boot… uh… I'm Wilbur Wilson."

"You have an associate, senor. Where is he?"

"Yeah, where's Dickey?" Phil asked, glancing around the hangar.

Booty swallowed hard.

"Umm, my associate… Richard… is… uh usin' the restroom. He'll be right out."

Paco's gaze shifted from Booty to Phil.

"And Caesar. Where is Caesar?"

Booty said nothing and looked at Phil.

"What the hell's going on?" Phil asked. "We need everyone here so we can get this done. Booty, go get Dickey outta the restroom, and I'll find Caesar."

Phil walked around the table and noticed a man's foot poking out from underneath a tarp on the floor. "What the fuck? Is that Caesar?"

"Let me explain," Booty said emphatically.

Paco stepped back and Phil pulled a pistol from his waistband and shot wildly towards the Mexicans, hitting Paco between the eyes. The tall man with the M4 returned fire hitting Phil three times, with two rounds going into his left shoulder and the third entering his left ear before exiting out the back of his head. Phil made no sound as he fell to the floor, eyes open.

Booty scrambled for the revolver tucked into his waistband as the tall man started to turn toward him, the rifle still in his shoulder. The gun got hung up on his belt, and Booty nearly dropped it to the floor before jerking it free and leveling at the tall man who already had a bead on him. This is it, Booty thought as his feet got tangled in the tarp, causing him to stumble just as the tall man squeezed the trigger.

Booty heard the shot, followed by two more, and was surprised that he felt no pain. His hands went to his face, head, neck, and chest. He looked at his hands, and there was no blood. Rolling to his right, he saw the tall man writhing on the floor, clutching his chest. Blood trickled from his mouth, and he was mouthing words without sound.

The sound of footsteps came near, and Booty reached for his revolver that was inches out of reach. He lunged for it, and the toe of a brown boot nudged it towards him. He looked up and saw Dickey.

"Get up, Wilbur. This ain't no time for a nap," Dickey said with a wild-eyed grin.

There was movement off to the left, and Booty watched Dickey draw the pistol from the holster on his hip and put a single shot into the tall man's forehead, ending his suffering.

"You okay, Wilbur?" Dickey asked.

Booty rose to his feet. "Hell no, I ain't okay! Look around, Dickey! Does this look okay? And don't call me Wilbur, goddammit. How many times do I got to tell you?"

Dickey shrugged. "What a mess huh?"

"A mess? It's a nightmare. Like something straight outta Greenfield."

"It surely is. I'm sorry about your buddy," Dickey said, motioning to Phil's body on the floor. "I never liked him much myself."

"He was always good to me," Booty responded.

Outside, a man with an M4 rifle stepped off the plane

and craned his ear towards the hanger. Booty and Dickey watched through the window as he talked into a walkie-talkie. The sound of a man speaking Spanish came from a walkie-talkie near them. It was in Paco's pocket. The man with the rifle started walking slowly towards the hangar, and the engine on the plane suddenly came to life.

"We gotta move, Booty," Dickie said as he darted towards the door. "Gather up the money and the dope. Go through everyone's pockets. Git the money and guns. Smash all the phones. I'll be back."

Booty didn't respond but went to work doing as Dickey said.

Outside, the man with the rifle stopped and looked nervously around. He spoke into the walkie-talkie again, got no response, turned, and ran back towards the plane.

The plane's engine revved as the man reached the steps.

From the hangar window, Dickey brought the Mini 14 into his shoulder and fired three rounds. The man fell, and Dickey raced from the hangar towards the plane. The pilot appeared at the top of the steps and attempted to close the door. Dickey fired a shot at the man but didn't hit him, and the man ducked inside.

Dickey dropped his rifle and drew his pistol while continuing towards the plane. He ran up the steps, stopped momentarily at the door, darted inside, crouched, and fired several shots toward the front of the aircraft.

The plane rolled forward as Dickey moved towards the cockpit. The pilot stood and lunged at Dickey.

"Motherfucker!" The pilot yelled.

Dickey and the pilot grappled as the plane veered off to the right, and slammed into a building. Both men fell to the floor. Dickey lost his grip on his pistol and saw it slide forward and under a seat, out of reach. The pilot grabbed at Dickey's face, gouging his eyes. He held Dickey's hair in both hands and slammed his head into the floor. Dickey tried to roll the pilot off, but the cramped space kept him pinned in place. The pilot punched Dickey hard in the center of his face, and Dickey saw stars. *I gotta do something,* Dickey thought. The pilot rose from his knees and went for Dickey's throat. When he did, Dickey slid his left hand up, found the pilot's testicles, and squeezed. The pilot writhed in pain and released Dickey's throat. With that, Dickey drew the hunting knife from its sheath, raised it behind the pilot's back, and brought it down three times in rapid succession, puncturing his kidney. The pilot screamed like a cat and tried to stand. Dickey pushed him away and rolled over on top of him. As the pilot struggled to get free, Dickey put his hand into the center of the pilot's face and pushed down as hard as he could. The pilot sensed his hopelessness and seemed to relax a bit as Dickey plunged the knife into the man's side, then brought it up to his throat and drove it all the way in, the tip contacting the floor beneath him. The pilot's eyes opened wide, and his arms and legs tightened momentarily, then relaxed. He gasped twice and then laid still and silent.

Dickey lay exhausted on the floor. Pain shooting through his head.

"That was a hell of a fight, my friend," Dickey said to the lifeless pilot. "You're a… well…was… You was a tough son of a bitch. Mighty tough."

"Dickey! Are you okay?" It was Booty.

Dickey sat up as Booty knelt beside him.

"How bad are you hurt," Booty asked.

"I ain't hurt," Dickey replied, spitting a tooth and a mouthful of blood onto the floor."

"Good thing you ain't hurt 'cause your right eye is damn near swelled shut."

Dickey grinned. "I feel like I been run over."

"We need to get movin'," Booty said.

Booty helped Dickey to his feet and retrieved his pistol from under the seat.

"Dickey," Booty said solemnly. "There's a hundred and sixty-six thousand dollars in cash, a pound of rock, a thousand Oxy, a shitload of weed, some coke, and the Lord only knows what else is in there. Plus, enough guns and ammo to arm a militia. We can go to Florida and retire."

"And sip drinks by the pool with the baby mamas, right?"

"That's right!"

They laughed as they walked off the plane and back towards the hangar.

Just then, a white Honda Accord drove through the gate and stopped as they approached the door. It was Du-Quayne and Marvin.

"Shit! Look who's back," Booty said.

Booty and Dickey were almost inside the hangar when Du-Quayne and Marvin saw them. Marvin stepped on the accelerator, and the Honda raced towards the hangar. Just as Booty closed the door behind them, Du-Quayne threw it open again.

"I'm gonna kill both of you mutha fuckas!" Du-Quayne yelled as he swung a ball bat at Booty.

Dickey drew his pistol and leveled it at Du-Quayne, who stopped in his tracks.

"You better use it, Dickey! Cause I'm fixin' to kill your ass!"

"Take it easy now, Du-Quayne. We were just funnin' about a little bit."

"Look at my face! Does that look like funnin' around to you? Fuckin tape tore my skin off!"

"I'm real sorry about that. I'm gonna put the gun down, and we'll work it out. Let me reimburse you for your troubles. How about five thousand dollars?"

The door opened, and Marvin walked in.

"And five thousand for Marvin, too. His face don't look too good either," Dickey continued.

"You gotta be fuckin' kiddin' me," Du-Quayne answered. He looked around the hangar at the bodies and out the window at the plane ran off the runway. "You done kilt all these damn Mexicans? Your ass is good as dead. They gonna hunt you down and skin you alive, boy. If I don't kill you first."

"You're pretty mad, huh?"

"Where's all the shit? Where's the money? That's all I care about."

"We got it all together. I'll tell you what. We'll cut you in. Ten percent. Take it and go."

"Fifty percent. Even split."

"Now, Du-Quayne. You know that ain't gonna happen. Me and Dickey worked hard for this, and we ain't just gonna give it up."

"I'll fight you for it, Dickey."

"Wooooo! Now, you're tempting me!"

"We got a deal?"

"I'll fight you for a split. You win, you get half. I win; we get it all. No weapons. Fight until one of us quits."

"You got a deal, hillbilly."

"Let's do it."

Dickey turned to Booty. "This ain't gonna take but a few minutes."

"Dammit, Dickey. Let's just take the shit and go. They ain't even got a gun. They can't stop us."

175

"That's probably the logical thing to do. But I hate that mother fucker."

"You're already beat half to death!"

"I've been wantin' to whip his ass since I seen him in Maysville. It won't take long."

"Fuck! I'm gonna get shit together. We'll take Phil's truck and put Du-Quayne's plates on it."

"Whatever you say, brother."

"Ring the bell, Marvin! Let's get it on!" Dickey yelled.

"Ding Dong, muthafucka!" Marvin said.

Dickey ran at Du-Quayne and tried to take him to the ground, but Du-Quayne slipped away and punched Dickey hard in the ribs, causing Dickey to grimace in pain.

They circled one another, both feigning punches while waiting for an opening. Finally, Du-Quayne tried to connect with a roundhouse right, but Dickey ducked under it and landed a hard right hand to Du-Quayne's stomach, doubling him over. Dickey followed up the punch with a knee to the center of Du-Quayne's face, opening up a gash in his upper lip and sending him sprawling to the ground.

Dickey tried to stomp Du-Quayne's face, but Du-Quayne rolled out of the way and staggered back to his feet.

"You having fun, city boy? This is playground shit in Greenfield."

"Shit. Your cracker ass wouldn't last five minutes a block south of Eight Mile. You be on a slab before you even know you dead."

The two circled one another, and Du-Quayne flicked out quick jabs with his right hand, causing Dickey's head to snap back.

'You ain't even see that, huh Dickey? One of these

dead Mexicans musta tuned your ass up before you killed him. That eye is swollen the fuck shut. Here, have another one."

Du-Quayne flicked out another quick right, but Dickey bobbed his head backward, causing him to miss. Suddenly, Dickey pivoted on his feet and started fighting left-handed to protect his swollen left eye.

"Look at you," Du-Quayne said. "You can fight right and left-handed. They call that something. Amber....? Shit, I can't remember."

"I learned it from watching Rocky," Dickey said proudly.

Du-Quayne swung hard, trying to end the fight with a wild haymaker. Dickey stepped back and let it go by before landing a hard shot to Du-Quayne's jaw and another to the middle of his face. Blood poured out of his nose. Dickey continued to batter Du-Quayne, dropping him to his knees.

"You're mine now, son of a bitch," Dickey snarled. "Welcome to Greenfield!"

Dickey kicked Du-Quayne in the face, sending him to the floor, and tried to follow it up with a stomp, but Du-Quayne rolled out of the way and sat up.

Dickey advanced, and when he did, Du-Quayne thrust out his right hand and sunk a three-inch blade into Dickey's right calf.

"You dirty bastard," Dickey muttered, clutching the wound. "You stabbed me. Now, I'm gonna kill ya."

Dickey kicked Du-Quayne hard in the side of the head, knocking him back down on the ground and causing him to drop the knife.

Booty rushed forward.

"No!" Dickey yelled.

Booty stopped in his tracks.

"Stay back. I got this," said Dickey.

Du-Quayne tried to get to his feet but couldn't. He took a feeble swipe at Dickey's legs. Dickey sidestepped it and got behind Du-Quayne.

"Lights out, asshole," Dickey whispered as he wrapped his arm around Du-Quayne's neck and pulled him tight against his body.

It only took a few seconds for Du-Quayne to quit struggling and a few more for him to stop breathing. Dickey released his hold and rolled away.

"I didn't want to kill him. I just wanted him to quit. Why'd he stab me?"

Suddenly, a loud crack split the air. Dickey winced and fell to the floor as a nine-millimeter slug ripped into his left shoulder.

"You didn't have to kill him, Dickey!" It was Marvin's voice, and he was moving in their direction.

Booty grabbed Dickey's rifle off the floor and scrambled for cover behind a wooden crate as Marvin squeezed off three more shots that missed their mark.

Dickey struggled to his knees as Marvin stopped beside him and pointed the gun at his head. "You ain't so bad now, are you, Dickey? Huntin ain't no fun when Marvin's got the gun, huh?"

"Put it down, Marvin!" Booty yelled.

When Marvin turned to look at Booty, Dickey kicked his hand, causing Marvin to fire a shot into the ceiling.

"Fuckin' Dickey," Marvin said, leveling his gun again at Dickey, who was now flat on his back.

Booty, knowing there was no other choice, squeezed the trigger of the Mini 14 and put a bullet through Marvin's left ear.

Marvin hit the floor and did not move.

"Dickey, we gotta get you to the hospital!" Booty

yelled.

"No time for that. Let's just go," Dickey said.

"You're hurt bad!"

Booty helped Dickey to his feet and grabbed the money bag. "Let's go, brother."

Sirens could be heard in the distance.

"The cops are coming," Dickey said.

Booty put an arm around Dickey and loaded him into Phil's truck. "No time to change plates. I'm afraid," Booty said. He put the money bag, drugs, and guns in the back, then ran to his truck and grabbed their bags.

"We gotta go, Booty!" Dickey yelled.

Booty jumped into Phil's truck, started the engine, and drove to the gate. He stopped momentarily, trying to decide from which direction the sirens were coming. Deciding they were coming from the left, he turned right onto the highway and sped away.

"How bad are you hurt, Dickey?"

Dickey was busy shredding his tee shirt and using the strips to bandage his leg and put pressure on his shoulder. "Well, that Mexican pilot about gouged my eyeball out, Du'Quayne put a knife in my leg, and Marvin, of all people, fuckin' shot me in the shoulder. Other than that? Hell, I'm good, Wilbur."

"Call me Wilbur one more time, and I'll dump your ass on the side of the road. I don't know where in the hell we are, but you need to go to the hospital."

"We ain't goin' to no hospital. They'll call the law the minute we walk through the door. We're goin' to Florida and find them baby mammas you're always blabbin' about."

"I'm not sure you'll make it, dammit."

"I will or I won't. That's fifty-fifty odds. Hell, I've bet on worse odds and won."

"You're so full of shit."

"Well, I won't argue against that. But I'm right. We ain't got no choice but to keep driving to Florida."

Booty said nothing.

Dickey looked at Booty and knew he was in deep thought. They were out of immediate danger, and now they just needed a plan. That's where Booty excelled, and Dickey knew that. So he let him think.

Finally, after several minutes, Booty spoke.

"Like I said, I don't know where we are. All I know is we gotta keep driving south. Eventually, we'll figure it out and get on our way. We need to stay off the interstates. Every cop in America will be looking for us there. We'll need a new license plate, so I'll pull over in some parking lot and switch one out. We'll go to the trailer park for a day or two. Get you patched up. Then we gotta get outta there. The cops probably don't know you and me were at that airport yet. But they'll figure it out and track down the parents cause they'll suspect that's where we went."

"Well," Dickey said. "If we can't stay permanent at the trailer park, where we gonna go then?"

"We'll have to go somewhere to hide. Start new lives, I guess. We got a shitload of money and plenty of drugs and guns we can sell to make more."

"You thinkin' Mexico?"

"Hell no. You been watchin' too many movies. I'm thinkin' someplace no one wants to go. Like Alabama. Or maybe Central America. We'd be rich as hell there. After that... I don't know."

"Sounds like a plan, Wil.... I mean Booty."

Booty nodded.

"You reckon there's baby mammas in them places?" Dickey asked.

"Are you serious?" Dicky answered, lighting a

cigarette. "Alabama's clear full of fine-looking baby mommas. Every shape, size, and color. I'm gonna git me a dark-haired shorty with big boobs and a bubble butt. We'll get you one of them skinny blondes you like. One with a missin' front tooth and a pot leaf tattoo on her ankle. How 'bout that, Dickey? You'd like that, wouldn't ya? Huh? Huh, Dickey? Dickey...?"

ONE DAY AT A TIME

"The Commandant of the Marine Corps has entrusted me to express his deep regret that your son, Corporal Mark Edward Morrow, was killed in action in Fallujah, Al Anbar, Iraq on 9 November 2004. At the time of his death, Corporal Morrow was leading a fire team of Marines against fortified enemy positions. Corporal Morrow's fire team came under mortar attack from insurgent forces hidden amongst civilians, and he was struck by shrapnel. He died instantly."

The words play in Ted Morrow's head like they're on a loop. Ten years ago today, and his heart remains broken.

Ted finishes off the Woodford Reserve in his glass and looks at the clock on the wall. Then he closes his eyes and buries his face in his hands. In the distance, a train whistle moans as it creeps through the dark, and a faraway dog answers its call. Train whistles are the opening riff to the soundtrack of Ted Morrow's life. Except for a few weeks thirty years ago, pitching for the Appleton Foxes, he has never lived more than a mile from the B&O Railroad in his fifty years. Ted ponders the fact and wonders if it means anything.

The 40-watt bulb in the table lamp casts a warm glow

across the corner of the room. It reminds Ted of when he and Lisa sat under a palm tree in Key West, drinking wine from the bottle and watching the last soft orange highlights of a hot summer day sink into the water. He loses himself in the thought, and a smile spreads across his face.

"One day at a time," Ted whispers, picking the revolver up from the desk and putting it back in the drawer. "One day at a time."

THE DEPRAVITY OF A MAN

The alarm goes off every morning at four - twenty. Most mornings, I am disappointed to wake up. I hit snooze once if I am taking a shower, twice if I am not, then I drag myself out of bed.

The dog follows me into the bathroom and waits for me to fill his water bowl. Then he drinks like he's not drunk in days. I stand at the toilet for two minutes, trying to take a piss. Why should something so simple be so difficult?

My wife and doctor have me on a shitload of pills for anxiety, high cholesterol, acid reflux, and God only knows what else. Neatly arranged doses in a plastic pill box with the days of the week printed on the lids. Some mornings, I take a fistful of them. Other mornings, I throw them in the trash.

If I am showering, I make the water as hot as I can take it and stand so it runs over my head. My thoughts turn to the nine-millimeter in the nightstand. Some mornings, when I am really disappointed, I consider slipping it out of the drawer and packing it with me so I can pull off into a field on the way to work and blow my brains out. Other mornings, I jerk off while fantasizing about the news lady from Fox News. The brunette with the legs. I don't remember her name.

I get out of the shower, dry off, and barely recognize the man looking back at me in the mirror. At fifty-four years old, I am closer to the end than I am to the beginning. What the hell happened?

Standing at the sink, I go through the ritual. Brush, floss, slap on some deodorant, and rub oil into my beard. Then I check my nose, ears, and eyebrows for stray hair, pop a couple Excedrin, and walk back into the bedroom.

My clothes lie folded on the dresser. I dress in the light coming through the crack in the bathroom door. My back hurts too bad to put my socks on while I stand, so I sit on the edge of the bed to do it. The wife rolls over and exhales her annoyance, so I get up and take my socks with me downstairs. The dog follows behind.

I walk into the kitchen, turn on the lights over the counter, and start the coffee pot. The dog dances with anticipation when he sees me reach for the cookie jar. Then, he runs to the back door and wags his entire ass while waiting for me to bring him one. I hand him a cookie, open the door, and watch him run off into the dark.

Socks in hand, I wander into the living room, sit down on the footstool, and put them on. My shoes are lying on the floor, so I slip my feet into them and remind myself again that the left one needs a new shoestring.

The dog stands on the back porch and barks because he's too spoiled to walk to the doggie door in the garage. I let him in, and he lies down by the fireplace.

The coffee maker beeps, and I walk back into the kitchen. I pour coffee into an old White Castle cup I bought a few years ago for fifty cents at a yard sale in

Blanchester. It's fifteen degrees outside, so I pop the steaming coffee in the microwave for twenty-two seconds to make it hot enough for the walk to my truck.

After putting on my coat, I walk outside, curse the cold, and think again of the nine-millimeter in the nightstand. I start my truck and pray there's gas in the tank. If there's not, I will stop at the Marathon station on the way out of town and curse the cold again.

As I drive by the Methodist Church, I go faster than I should by the herd of pricks running four abreast down the middle of the dark street, ignoring the sidewalks on either side. They yell, "Slow down, asshole!"

I flip them the finger and respond with "Fuck you!" This scene plays out verbatim nearly every morning.

I drive to work and ponder every success I have had and every failure I have endured over the past thirty-five years. I cycle through a multitude of what-ifs like I am reading them from a checklist, and wonder if it's too late to change course. I listen to obscure music from Wayne Hancock, Ruthie Foster, and Old 97's and wonder why such talented musicians never made it, but shitty acts like U2 and Taylor Swift became superstars. Occasionally, I listen to a true-crime podcast and ponder what it means when I empathize with the killer. Some mornings, I drive the entire 32.2 miles in silence and don't remember a single detail of the trip.

I pull through the gate and fake smile at the sad looking guy in the guard shack. "Good morning, Mr. Connor," he says.

I stare hard at his name tag and say, "Hello, Marty. How are you this morning?" It almost sounds like I care.

As I park my truck in front of the sign with my name stenciled on it, I am struck by the fact that my depravity goes largely unnoticed in the real world. I am a tiny speck of nothing on a minuscule grain of sand hurtling through endless emptiness. Here though, I am the boss. I have the answers. I play my part. I have an intern who brings me coffee. I have an overpaid staff that tells me what I want to hear, and an underpaid assistant that tells me what I need to hear. I schedule meetings so I can listen to myself talk, while those seated around me nod and pretend to take notes. I pay others to make mistakes so I can tell them how to fix them.

Tomorrow, I will do it all again.

BILL STUMLOSKI DOES NOT TAKE
PRISONERS

Bill Stumloski sits in the dark, drinking coffee and staring at the window. Laying across his lap is a Mosin Nagant rifle, with a round chambered and the bayonet attached. The window is cracked a few inches, and the curtains move gently in the breeze. He can hear the sounds of summer drifting through the air. Not the pleasant sounds of crickets chirping, kids playing, and whistles from slow-moving trains. These summer sounds are more ominous: men arguing, glass breaking, women screaming, and sirens wailing.

Bill looks at his watch but can't make out the time in the dark. *It's past midnight*, he guesses. *Zero one, zero two, maybe.* He thinks about having a cigarette. Then he remembers that he hasn't smoked since coming home from Korea seventy years ago.

Those were the days. Second Battalion, First Marines. The Professionals. Chesty Puller, Inchon, Seoul, Chosin Reservoir. Bill thinks of Baker, Gullett, Big Tex, and Little Tex. He thinks of Irish Mike McAdams and remembers how Mike went to take a piss one night, and the North Koreans grabbed him.

They wrapped him in barbed wire, doused him with gasoline, lit him on fire, and rolled him down a hill in front of their position. Bill covered his ears until Mike's cries for his mother became a whimper as the sun came up. Finally, Mike was still. Bill vowed never to take a prisoner after that, and he meant it.

There are two of them. A tall, skinny, white trash-looking piece of shit and a short, fat, one-eyed Guatemalan. Bill has seen them walking past his house many times before, always staring. Sometimes they stand on the corner talking, pointing, and looking guilty. One day, a few weeks ago, they stopped while Bill was watering his rose bushes, and the white trash one said, "Hey, old man, give me twenty dollars."

Bill gave them a hard stare instead, and they cussed at him and walked away.

They stole the table and chairs from under the tree in the front yard. They cut the hose Bill used to water his flowers and broke the cement ducks that had sat in the yard every summer since he and Mary had moved from Greenfield to Dayton in the early Seventies. Mary loved those ducks, and it infuriates him that they are gone. They took the bulb from the porch light one day last week, and every time he replaces it, they take it again.

Four days ago, Bill noticed damage around his front door where they had tried to jimmy it. That's when he started leaving the window cracked.

Thanks to the Marines, Bill has a plan. He has sat in the dark living room for three nights and stared at that window, but nothing has happened. He never sleeps anyway, so it isn't a big deal. He'll be ready when the time comes.

On the fourth night, Bill sees them sneaking across the yard and up to the house. He thinks maybe it's the bastards that killed Irish Mike, but it's White Trash and

One Eye instead.

Bill lifts the rifle slowly and waits. White Trash pushes open the window, slithers in like a snake, and stands up. Bill's view is blocked, but he can hear grunting and thumping as White Trash pulls One Eye into the window. Bill puts the rifle into his shoulder, welds his cheek to the stock, and waits patiently for White Trash to step back, which he does.

Bill stops breathing momentarily, places the front sight post over the top of One Eye's head, and squeezes the trigger. There's a flash and a loud crack. It's the first angry sound the rifle has made since he brought it home from Korea in 1952.

One Eye lies motionless, half in and half out the window. White Trash screams and tries to jump outside, but One Eye does his job and blocks the way. Bill calmly chambers another round and slides up to the edge of his recliner. He squeezes the trigger again, and White Trash flies forward into the wall and falls on top of his friend.

Bill stands up and walks across the room. He stops at the pile of bodies and nudges them with the toe of his shoe. *Sure enough,* he thinks, *these are the bastards that got Irish Mike.* The one on the bottom is dead, but the one on top moans, so Bill places the point of the bayonet in the soft spot at the base of the man's skull and pushes. The man whimpers a little, then becomes quiet.

Bill Stumloski does not take prisoners.

THE STREETS OF GREENFIELD

"If you wanna know about Greenfield, sit down, and I'll tell ya all about it. As long as Pearl doesn't run out of coffee, I'm all yours."

"Start from the beginning? What beginning? I'm only eighty-five years old, son. I can take you back to the mid-forties, and most of what I'll tell you is the truth. If you want anything before that, I'll tell you what I've heard, or I'll make something up. Deal?"

"Pearl, darlin'. Can you bring me a fresh cup and a hard roll? Thanks, sweetie. Warm that roll up a little."

"I remember when Pearl was the best lookin' woman within a hundred miles of Greenfield. Big jugs, long legs, beautiful face, bright blue eyes, and bleach blonde hair. She was a looker! She got into the hippie shit in the late sixties, early seventies. Rode out west with that Delaney boy. The funny one. Morris. Yeah, Morris Delaney. He was funny, but he grew up on the south end of town, so he wasn't no sissy. No, sir. Tough as shoe leather. Had to be, growing up down there. Pearl came back to town after a few months and started settling down. Delaney stayed out there, though. Last I heard, he was in Montana or

191

Wyoming. Some shit like that."

"Thanks, Pearl."

"You should try one of these rolls. Pearl makes em from scratch. Best hard roll I've had outside of New Jersey."

"I was eleven years old when I saw Bill Niles get shot and killed on South Second Street back in 1949. Seen it with my own eyes. With God as my witness. Two shots in the back as he walked by old man Connor's Store in broad daylight. I was sitting in the fork of a maple tree in front of Frank Platt's house on the corner of Summerfield and Second. The tree is gone now. Anyway, I was sitting in the tree trying to look at a robin's nest when old Bill came staggering down the sidewalk on the other side of the street. He was drunk, of course. Bill stayed drunk. And he was singing "Filipino Baby" at the top of his lungs. Three men in a dark green Ford pulled up beside him, and the man in the back seat shot him. The car drove off like nothing happened. Kept going down Second Street, across the tracks, and towards the old red bridge. The killers were never caught."

"You can't really understand Greenfield unless you were born and raised here. It's in your blood. It's part of you, just like your thumbprint. You can leave, move away, and pretend to forget Greenfield, but you'll never get it out of you. It's always home, and something will draw you back in time. Maybe just for a little while. But you'll be back. Hell, I moved to Circleville in 1963. Took a job at a factory up there making canteen covers for the Army. I stood at a table putting brass snaps on those covers for nine hours a day. Hated it. My fingers never stopped hurting. Worked three months before I quit and took a job in Mount Sterling, helping build the new post office. It was a government contract, so they had us work as slowly as possible. Laziest bunch of sons-a-bitches I've ever seen in my life. I lasted ten days, then hitchhiked back to Greenfield. Got a job at the slaughterhouse workin' in the hog pens. That was the hardest job I ever had. I was home, though, so I didn't mind it as much. I stayed there for ten years, then went to work at the textile factory. That's where I retired from. I was there when Jerry Garner was plant manager. You ever hear about Jerry? He ran hookers outta that place for fourteen years. Made a fortune. Man, what a time…"

"Back in the old days, they called Greenfield Little Chicago. It was a rough place then. I guess it still is today in some ways, but it was different then. You had to act tough, even if you wasn't. How you walked and how you talked was important. Even how you dressed. You had to know how to bluff. If that didn't work, you had to use your fists. That's why Greenfield has always had so many tough guys. I mean legitimate tough guys. Real ass kickers."

"There musta been thirty beer joints in town in the fifties and sixties. Even into the seventies. The Diamond Grill, Ponchos Pub, The Village Pump, The Huddle, The Pad Cafe, Johnny's Eight Ball, The Guest Room... Always trouble. Guys pissin' on the sidewalk, fights, sirens blaring all night long."

"Ruthie Sims owned a place on Jefferson Street where McDonald's is now. The sign over the door said "MacArthur Inn," but everyone called it "Ruthie's Place." Towards the end of every month, just before the welfare checks came out, two guys from Lucasville would park their car in the alley behind the bar. Ruthie's son, Paulie, cocky little bastard with a Hollywood flattop, would come out and run two hoses from the car's boot through the back window of the bar and fill twenty empty bottles with moonshine. Twenty more were filled halfway and topped off with grape Kool-Aid. Ruthie sold the Straight Shine for four dollars a bottle and the Grape Shine for two - fifty. The town drunks loved it."

"Around 1958, or maybe 59, Bob Connor and his brother Doyle got jumped by four guys from Ripley while walking home from the pool hall. They got em in the alley that runs by Tucker's Restaurant. You see, Bob had taken all their money playin' pool, and they were hell bent on gettin' it back. Well, let me tell you what. Bob and Doyle commenced to whippin' them boy's asses. Put three of em in the hospital. The only thing that was bruised on Bob and Doyle was their knuckles. They didn't even call the police. Just walked home and left them boys layin' in the alley."

"I don't know whatever happened to Doyle, but Bob is still around town. He's a few years older than me, but I got to runnin' around with him around the time they kicked them guy's asses." One morning, Bob showed up at my front door, grinning like his ship had just come in. It was October 1, 1965. I remember the date because it was the day before his son, Jack, was born. Bob had two Thompson submachine guns and a case of twenty-four Mk 2 grenades, the old pineapple kind, in the boot of his car. He got em for next to nothing from a guy who had stolen them while he was stationed at Fort Benning. The guy had kept them hidden in his parent's garage over on Spring Street for two years and just wanted to offload them. Bob gave him seventy bucks for the lot, then paid me fifteen to ride down to Knockemstiff so he could sell the guns and grenades to some guys he met at a card game in Roxabel. They was probably in the Klan, but who knows? Anyway, we drove his dad's 1947 Chevy panel truck to Knockemstiff and parked outside this old country store on Route 50. We expected some barefoot toothless clodhoppers to show up. Instead, we met with two men that coulda passed for Ward Cleaver. They were smiling and polite, the same as if they were buying a bouquet of roses for their girls. I was sitting in the passenger side with a Winchester Model 12 in my lap while Bob made the sale. Honestly, I felt a little foolish. We left with four hundred dollars cash, ten cases of Kentucky bourbon, and a hundred cartons of cigarettes. Bob was good enough to give me a bottle of bourbon and two packs of smokes as a bonus for helping him out. That was Honest Bob's last big adventure. After that, Helen put him on notice and made him get a real job. Clipped his wings, you might say."

"By the early seventies, Greenfield was so wild that Bill Stumloski moved his family to Dayton to escape it. Can you believe that? Outside of Gary, Indiana, Dayton, Ohio, might be the biggest shithole in the Midwest. Bill thought it was safer than Greenfield, though. Go figure."

"See that guy that just came in the door? That's Samuel Sommers. His nickname growing up was Four-Eyed Opie. Man, he could hit a baseball. Went to Texas after college forty-some years ago. Moved back to Greenfield when his mom died a couple years back. Quiet guy. Kinda odd, but doesn't bother anyone."

"What's that? A chip? Would I say Greenfield has a chip on its shoulder? Why, heavens, yes. People here carry their chip in their front pocket and plop on their shoulder as needed. It's really an inferiority complex, but no one would ever admit that. You see, people from the bigger towns in the area all looked down on Greenfield. Chillicothe, Washington Court House, Hillsboro, Wilmington. All county seats. The U.S. highways ran through them, so they grew more than Greenfield did.

They built shopping centers, and then the fast-food joints opened up. Greenfield didn't have any of that stuff. We had McClain High School, though. Yeah, old Edward Lee McClain did us right. That school is like an art gallery and an Ivy League Museum rolled into one. None of the county seats around here had a school that even came close. That made them jealous and caused them to treat us with even more contempt. That's why Greenfield has an attitude. Notice I didn't say that people from Greenfield have an attitude. I said that Greenfield has an attitude. And it's rightly earned. There's attitude in the dirt. It's in the water. It's in the air. Man, it lives in every building, every tree, and in every headstone on every grave in every boneyard in town. We ain't ashamed of it either. People that lived and died before I was even born earned it. And us younger folks? It's our birthright. Watch us when we walk. Listen to us when we talk. You can't miss it."

"You ever go to a McClain Tigers football game? The place is packed. Standing room only. Why is that? Is it because McClain is winning so many championships? Hell no! McClain ain't won fifty games in the last twenty-five years. It's the attitude! That's Greenfield's team! You think Greenfield's team is gonna play Washington Court House or Hillsboro, and the people ain't coming out for it? We put our purple and gold on and strut around like the kings of the Earth. I've seen seventy-year-old men stand around that football field and cry when the fight song is played, or on them rare occasions when the victory bell is rung. No, sir, it ain't just about football. It's pride in something. Something you couldn't possibly understand unless you were born and raised here."

"Listen; let me leave you with this. Greenfield is a tough place. That much is well documented. It's not all we are, though. We're decent people. Most of us, anyway. Paulie Sims, the cocky kid that filled the moonshine bottles. He quit high school and joined the Army. Went to Vietnam with the 82nd Airborne. Came home and started his own carpentry business. Does great work. Six years ago, I slipped on the ice and broke my hip. Spent three weeks in the hospital. When I got home, I called Paulie to build me a ramp so I could get in and out of my house. He came over the day after I got home and built that ramp. Took him all day. I went to pay him, and he told me he'd mail me an invoice. I kept looking for it in the mail, but it never came. I called him a dozen times, and he always said he'd "get that in the mail tomorrow." That was six years ago. I still ain't never got an invoice. That's Greenfield."

"Bob Connor's boy, Mike. Nicest guy I've ever known. Take's after his mom. He bought King Sheik's barber shop down on the corner of Second and Paint thirty-some years ago. You know, his shop is the happiest place in town. Whenever I go in for a haircut, I laugh so much my ribs hurt. Mike buys a truck full of hams every year just before Christmas and drops them off on people's porches who might need them. Just a generous guy. That's Greenfield."

"And then, there's Pearl. The gal that's been filling our coffee cups for the last two hours. Like me, she's never been married. Not for lack of offers, either. She could have married any man in town. Hell, I'd marry her right now. She has a dozen rental properties around Greenfield. Takes good care of em. Nice clean places. Keeps them affordable for working people. Well, there used to be a man in town named Emo Gotlieb. He was Polish and had been in a concentration camp during World War Two. Somehow, he ended up in Greenfield.

No one ever knew why or how. Just showed up one day. Emo scratched out a living, picking up pop bottles and doing odd jobs. Then he got old and couldn't get around anymore. Had no money. No family. Nothing. Pearl put him in a nice little house on Lafayette Street, a block from downtown. Charged him five dollars a month rent because Emo wouldn't take charity. He lived there for several years. Then he died there.

Pearl paid for his funeral, and she decorates his grave every Memorial Day. That's Greenfield."

"Friend, I've given you a lot but left a lot out, too. We didn't talk about Duncan MacArthur, Admiral Noble Irwin, C.R. Patterson, General John E. Hull, Red Armstrong, Don Grate, or Pat Massey and The Massey System. Nor did we mention Allen Delaney, Johnny Paycheck, Con Yoder, Fiona Farmer, Booty Wilson, Dickie Dance, or Tom Allen. You can go to the library and read about them, though. They're all there. Famous and infamous alike. Or better yet, you can ask other folks about them. Don't get it all from me. Fact-check me. You'll see that what I'm telling you is true. Most of it, anyway."

"Greenfield is unique. Unlike anyplace else I've ever been. She's my hometown, and I love her. The good. The bad. The beauty. The scars. It is what it is."

"It's been good talking with ya, son. Good luck with whatever you're working on. Maybe you oughta write a book about this little town. It might be a bestseller.".

THE DANCE OF THE SHADOW PEOPLE

It was a little past two a.m. and my ear was pressed to the thin wall that separated my apartment from the empty one next door. The voices had started around midnight, whispering in starts and stops. I could hear them but I couldn't determine what they were saying. I could almost make it out. It was like I knew what the voices were saying, but I forgot what they said once I tried to analyze it. You could bet it wasn't good, though. Otherwise, they wouldn't be whispering.

If they wanted to get together, they'd knock on my door and say, "Hey man, we've got some cream and need a place to party. Can we use your dump?"

"Sure," I'd have said, "Come on in. No needles, though. Needles are for common tweakers. I can't have that here." Then they'd have pulled their bubbles from their pockets, and I would have invited them in.

I hadn't slept a wink in three days. My focus, before the whispering started, had been on smoking meth, masturbating, disassembling, and reassembling my ancient record player, scouring my kitchen sink, and carpet surfing for tiny pieces of rock I may have dropped.

All this whispering shit meant trouble. Four words kept running through my head: *Coming to get me.*

I grabbed my keys off the table and headed for the door. I wasn't wearing shoes, but I didn't need them. *Too heavy,* I thought. *They'd weigh me down.* I opened the front door slowly. So slowly that it was hard to detect any movement at all. Then I listened. There it was. Singing. Like a church choir. I couldn't make out the song, but they were singing. I looked up and down the street for cops and made sure no one was looking out of the empty apartment's windows or hiding behind the bushes. Why didn't the landlord cut those damn things down? The singing came from the neighbor's backyard, so I walked across the street, past their garage, and through the gate. I could still hear it, but now it was coming from across the back fence. This is how it always went. For six months, I had chased that freaking choir all over the neighborhood but could never get any closer, no matter how hard I tried. They were constantly moving and always singing.

I walked back through the yard, out the gate, past the garage, and across the street. I stood next to my car, scanning the area. My feet were wet from the damp grass, and sand and grit stuck to the bottoms, so I wiped them on my pant legs. All the while, I never took my eyes off my apartment door. The humming from the streetlamp was trying to drown out the church choir that sounded like it was coming back this way. How could anyone sleep with all that noise?

The lights flashed when I unlocked the car doors, and I froze. Then, I slowly opened the door and peeked into the back. It was empty. So, I slid into the seat and started the engine. Nice and quiet. That was good. It was quiet because I took care of my shit. Oil changed and filter replaced. Fluids topped off. Tires rotated, balanced, and aligned. Washed and waxed. My dad taught me that. I checked the mirrors and flipped on the left turn signal before pulling out and heading down Lyndon Avenue.

I was creeping slowly past Fifth Street when I saw the first shadow man. They were always men. He rose up behind a car parked on the street. Ten feet tall. Maybe twelve. One arm fanning the night air. *Ride on through!* He had no face, but he would be grinning if he did. Not a friendly grin, but a toothy, menacing grin. You know the kind of grin I'm talking about. A grin like that clown in the Stephen King movie has. I drove slowly past and watched the shadow man fold into the ground and disappear. In the rearview mirror, I saw him rise back up from the pavement and twist around to watch me drive away.

As I drove, the shadow people popped up from underneath parked cars, out from behind trees, and up from sewer grates. They danced their dance, like those inflatable tube men you see at car lots. Bending at the waist, then straightening up, arms waving frantically. Some wore top hats that they tipped before sinking back into the ground.

Three days without sleep, and things were beginning to make sense. Everything was coming into focus. You know what I'm saying, right? The whispering, the church choir, the shadow people. It meant something. I'd discussed it before, but no one else seemed to understand. They all said I was spun out. Yeah, I was spun out, but that's how you come to understand these things.

I turned left onto Washington Street, then cut into the big gravel lot between the railroad tracks and what used to be the lumber company, Waddell's showcase factory, and the old feed mill. Shadow people popped out from under the buildings, then folded into the ground as I passed. Others rose from the rooftops and floated into the dark sky like dead spirits. One approached me along the railroad tracks from the direction of the trestle over Paint Creek. He must have been thirty feet tall. I stopped my car and put it in Park while the shadow man marched towards me, lifting his legs high with deliberate steps like he was walking on fly paper. He shrank as he came closer and was no taller than me when he stood in front of the car, bathed in the bright white from the headlights.

I climbed out of the car and walked toward him, the sharp gravel digging into my bare feet. The church choir started up again, and although I wasn't sure, I think they were singing "How Great Thou Art." It gave me confidence as I approached the shadow man who did not retreat into the dusty gravel, if you can believe it.

This is where the story gets a little weird. I stood face to face with the shadow man, except the shadow man had no face. He had no layers. He had no depth at all. He was two-dimensional. For a moment, I felt his warm breath on my face, but how could that be? I sensed the shadow man wanted to tell me something, although he gave me no reason to think that. I tried to channel his thoughts, but all I heard was the choir as their song built to its crescendo. The shadow man did not move. I tried to imagine he had eyes, and I looked into the space where they might be if he did have them. "Are you trying to tell me something?" I asked.

There was no response.

"Are you trying to communicate with me?" I spoke slowly and loudly like I might to someone who didn't speak English in an effort to force them to understand.

I remembered my high school Spanish teacher, Mrs. O'Toole, leaning on my desk, her face inches from mine, wagging a pencil with her gnarled fingers. "¿Qué es esto, Pablo?" The sour odor of cigarettes and black coffee emanated from her mouth, thick and heavy, strong enough to gag a maggot. She spoke slowly, and her dry lips formed every syllable. Her enunciation was excellent. Her pronunciation perfect. "¿Qué es esto, Pablo?"

"¡Es un lápiz, señora!" I shouted at the shadow man. "If you are trying to communicate with me, I'm not getting it. Are you trying to communicate with me?" My lips formed every syllable. "Are you try-ing to tell me some-thing im-por-tant? If so, I am not get-ting it," I said with a shrug.

In the distance, the church choir started to sing another song. The grand finale. "The Battle Hymn of The Republic," perhaps. I began to crash and feared an ear ringer was coming on. I needed to get home.

The choir sang louder, and the shadow man started to move. He moved his torso. Then he moved his shoulders. Then he raised his arms over his head, and he danced. Bending at the waist, first to the left, then to the right. Then standing erect with his arms raised over his head. He danced the dance of the shadow people!

As I drove away, I could see him in the glow of my taillights, gyrating to the rhythm of a tune only he could hear.

When I returned to my apartment, it was finally clear what the shadow man was trying to communicate. It was the dance! He wanted the people to dance! So, I put a record on the turntable, and while I waited for the needle to finish its staticky prelude, I filled my bubble with the crumbs of rock, pieces of lint, and multicolored cat hair harvested from my carpet. Then, I smoked.

As the vapor filled my lungs and the euphoria filled my head, Frank Sinatra sang "Strangers in The Night," and I danced the dance of the shadow people!

THE DAYS WERE LONGER THEN

Sometimes, when the sun hits my face just right, and I allow the warmth to envelop me, I go back beyond twenty thousand yesterdays and lie in the grass looking up at the clouds. My mother's voice calls me to supper, and her face, so young, decades younger than I am now, looks down at me and smiles.

The scent of lilac through an open window, the smoothness of a well-worn coin in my hand, a creaking floorboard beneath my feet, a rustling newspaper, a whiff of aftershave, Patsy Cline on the radio. Reminders, calling out through the white noise of time.

The memories rest in my soul where the vibrant colors are tinged with sepia tones, and the reels play at three-quarters speed. Layers of family surrounded me. The laughter, the songs we sang, the voices echoing through the years. The days were longer then. The water was cooler, the trees taller, and six blocks from home in any direction was another world.

Summer afternoons in my granny's kitchen. White tee shirts, gym shoes, and Wrangler jeans. Friends moving in and friends moving out. Sharing a room with my big brother, Mike. Backyard campouts, fishing in Paint Creek, baseball games in the feed mill lot. Walking along the B&O, picking up pop bottles, and trading them in at the store for candy. The sting of an ice-cold RC Cola against the back of my throat, stealing Camels and Luckies from the old man's car, and riding bicycles we built from junk. I can still smell the tar on Second Street and feel how soft it was beneath my shoes.

I remember my first kiss, the scent of her dime-store perfume, and the taste of her lips. I dreamed it would last forever. It lasted most of the summer instead.

Drinking warm beers under the trestle with my best friend, Bob, and hearing "Hey Jude" for the first time on my brother's transistor radio. Thinking of the future. Wishing and wanting, and coming to the realization that I was poor.

Lying in bed and feeling the loneliness from the whistle of a slow-moving train. The smell of fresh-cut hay and long days at the lake. Friday night football games. Coming out of the locker room as the band played our fight song, Fight the team across the field. Show them McClain is here! Looking into the stands and seeing her looking back.

Sitting on the roof of the high school and watching the cars drive by. Sneaking into the Ranch Drive-In. Running wide open in the old man's GTO. Driving on empty and hoping I'd make it home.

Watching her move and noticing the way her hair fell around her face. Turning around and seeing her walk away. Too much wine and not enough time. Not enough time.

Somehow, I missed the moment when my youth slipped away. Dreams faded, and reality rushed in to fill the void they left behind. Love came and went and came again, just like the seasons. Finally, a son was born, and love became a family of three.

One late summer day, I found myself in a field filled with flowers and granite stones. I stood alone while surrounded by others. Life seemed to stop. Then, an old love became new. It felt seamless, and I started to live again.

I still walk the streets of my youth from time to time. They are narrower now, and the trees are not as tall as they were then. On occasion, though, when the sun hits my face just right and I allow the warmth to envelop me, I can hear the laughter and the faint echoes of days gone by. Sometimes, my old friend Bob, gone for many years, walks with me. I sense him there, and if the shadows line up perfectly, I can see him out of the corner of my eye. Goofy grin, letterman's jacket, penny loafers, a fleeting whiff of a cigarette. I'm careful not to turn my head his way for fear of upsetting the shadows. I just talk, and I ask him if he remembers. Sometimes he laughs, and other times, when it's very quiet and a soft breeze blows ever so gently, I'm almost sure I can hear him cry. Mostly though, he listens. He listens.

Eric Grate

ACKNOWLEDGMENTS

My sincere thanks to:

My family for making the time for me to write this book.

The staff at Big Jack's, especially Megan, Savannah, and Hannah, for running things without me and never missing a beat.

The people who have encouraged and supported me from day one.

My coffee maker for never letting me down.

The people of Greenfield, Ohio. The toughest people I have ever known in my life. God bless you all.

Eric Grate